T0209954

# SOMETIMES

JOEL BERNARD

authorHOUSE®

*AuthorHouse™ LLC*
*1663 Liberty Drive*
*Bloomington, IN 47403*
*www.authorhouse.com*
*Phone: 1-800-839-8640*

*Published by AuthorHouse 11/13/2013*

*ISBN: 978-1-4918-1089-7 (sc)*
*ISBN: 978-1-4918-1087-3 (hc)*
*ISBN: 978-1-4918-1088-0 (e)*

*Cover design and cover illustration by Eben Swanson*

*Library of Congress Control Number: 2013914988*

*This book is printed on acid-free paper.*

*I oftentimes would hang by my knees from the gym bars on the playground. The blood rushing to my head calmed me; being upside down also gave a new perspective to life. It made it more understandable, more accepting, more exciting; the distortion made us more alike than different ...*

Sometimes I wonder where my place is in this time we call life. It is not that I feel less confused than others about my role in the world or that I believe I have been placed on this Earth to fulfill some destiny that God has designed; the truth of the matter is I believe in neither God nor destiny. Perhaps it is my misgivings about human beings in general that causes me to consider my inevitable destruction by my own hand. When I was ten years old, I was told to go kill myself. Cecilia, a classmate, screamed those words into my face while tears streamed down her cheeks. I do not remember what caused her sudden burst of anger; nor did I have any insight into the dilemma it provoked. But her words remain with me to this day.

Cecilia's words, although those of a child, burned themselves permanently into my consciousness, as undeniably as if done so with a branding iron; it is difficult, as I walk through life, not to be reminded of those words. A child's scream, a dog's bark, a car horn—anything really—can cause my mind to spin wildly; a computer gone mad, it gyrates until it stops on that fateful sequence of words. I rarely break out in a sweat-any longer and seldom if ever begin to tremble as I once did. I fear I have come to accept the curse and its consequences as one accepts the chicken pox.

I sometimes wonder what Cecilia might look like today. As I recall, she was taller than the rest of my classmates, including me, and outweighed us by a good forty pounds. She wasn't fat as I remember; big boned is what people said. She had short, cropped hair, a bowl cut. Her size was accentuated by the dresses she wore; they looked several sizes too small. She filled them like a potato sack bursting at the seams. She was, as my companions referred to her, a *lunker*. She wasn't pretty or ugly. She was a girl, and girls at the age of ten were just things we did not understand. There were boys, dogs, baseball, and things in dresses. Life was so much simpler then.

I would not have given any credence to the fact that I'd been cursed by those fateful words had it not been for Ralph's insistence that his dog died seconds after having crossed paths with Cecilia. They were on their way to the park when she stepped from behind a tree. The dog turned in fright according to Ralph and never saw the car that "popped him like a balloon."

The curse, no doubt, was real, and I must admit, I have been looking for an antidote ever since. Antidotes are rare. I have looked in libraries and bookstores and talked to religious historians, and as of yet, I cannot say I've made any progress. Ralph said that was because the curse is so powerful others won't risk the consequences of retaliation by discussing it. I have to be honest; I thought that he was "full of crap" as we were fond of saying—that is until Ralph was hit by a car on the way home from school, dead, gone. Lisa, Ralph's sister, said it was the same car that had killed their dog, and after that she refused to leave the block, most days the house.

Butcher, my best friend, says it's all too coincidental to be anything but fate. Butcher is difficult to understand at times.

"How'd she know it was the same car if the car didn't stop?" Butcher asked, more out of a sense of obligation than inquisitiveness.

"She said it was the license plate."

"What did it say?" he asked in his annoyingly ambiguous tone.

"His sister said that it simply read, PIG 63."

"Was she sure?" Butcher yawned. "I know that plate."

"You know that plate?" I found myself responding like a doll whose string had been pulled. Butcher looked concerned. It wasn't like Butcher to look concerned or even reasonably interested. His expression began to frighten me. Perhaps there was something to this curse after all.

"That plate, PIG 63, belongs to my granddad. What do you think of that?" Butcher crouched down and looked me right in the eye.

I hadn't even realized I'd sat down until then, must have been the shock. "You sure?" I questioned skeptically.

Butcher was prone to exaggeration and, at times, outright fabrication.

"Of course, I'm sure. My granddad was a pig farmer in Iowa, and after he lost all his money—at least that's what my mom says—he had to come live with us or they were going to put him in a home or have him put to sleep. Maybe it was his dog they were going to put to sleep. I can't really remember all the details. It was a long time ago, last year I think. Anyway, he has a Cadillac—purple, with the license plate PIG 63 right there on the rear bumper. You'd remember the car if you saw it; he painted it himself. We still have the purple swatches on the driveway to prove it." Butcher sat with his eyes on the ground, shaking his head in disbelief. "Hard to believe that my granddad has killed a dog and one of our buddies and that it doesn't have something to do with the curse. My granddad has a hard time parking in our driveway; I'm surprised he could actually manage to hit a dog. You don't suppose we got this all wrong and that the curse was on the dog, do you?"

"Well then, what about Ralph?" I added just for the sake of argument.

It's difficult not to believe in curses. I think it's because life is simpler when we can blame our misfortunes on something we can't control. Butcher says it wasn't my fault; Cecilia was just taking it out on me because she had to take it out on someone. It's not her fault either, he says. She was just big for her age, different, and kids who are different get picked on and teased. I guess I can understand all that, but if it's not my fault and it's not her fault and it's not Butcher's fault, then whose fault is it? Butcher says it's nobody's fault. It's just the way things are, like a dog is a just a dog.

I don't know if I buy all that stuff. When Cecilia put her face within a few inches of mine and screamed, "Go kill yourself," I did feel it was my fault. I didn't mean to hurt her feelings. I don't even remember ever saying anything to her about her size. I don't ever remember saying anything to her at all, ever. But then, if that is true, why do I feel so guilty? I can't help feeling it is my fault. I can't help feeling that I must have done something to cause her to say those words to me. I can't help feeling that her words haunt me, crawling around in my dreams like a worm in an apple, that her words do have power over me.

If you put your hand in the fire, you get burned. Being burned is the consequence of placing your hand in the fire. If you jump off a building and land on the concrete below, you will turn into something resembling a smashed pumpkin. The consequence of jumping is pumpkin. So, if I did something that I am guilty of, whether or not I meant it, or even knew I was responsible for it, then would the consequences be the curse?

Butcher says that's all bull—that guilt and consequence are not related. "If guilt and consequence were related, there would be no need for God."

I had to ask him to explain. I failed to make the connection between guilt, consequence, and God.

"Simple," he said, "if there is a connection between guilt and consequence, then there would be no need for God. God is the middleman, don't you see. He's like the traffic cop with that stupid little sign and whistle. Blow the whistle, you go, you stop; it's all on Him. He has the control. He has the ability to change your guilt to innocence. But it's all up to you. You have to ask."

Butcher, at times, amazed me. Sometimes, I looked at him and didn't see a kid, but an old man in kid's clothes. I can't help but wonder if that is part of the curse, altered perception. "So, where did you get this crap?"

Butcher stiffened. "Sunday School man. Where else? That Mrs. Johnson can put the fear of God in anyone, believe me. You should come with sometime. I know you Catholics think old Martin Luther was a rebel because he refused to worship the Pope, but believe me, the Pope is small potatoes compared to Mrs. Johnson."

Butcher belonged to some after church group where the kids got together on Thursdays I think it was. They apparently talked about all sorts of things, and it seemed like very few of them had to do with theology. He was convinced that, if we elected a Catholic president, the Pope was coming over to run America. He said his folks were working hard to see that didn't happen. His yard was full of sticks with signs on them. It looked like a flower garden for the insane. But there was no talking to Butcher about it, so I quit trying. He could be more than stubborn if he set his mind to it. The Pope, he said, made everyone at church group real nervous.

It is difficult to argue with logic as straightforward and disciplined as Butcher's, so I no longer try. He did have a point though. Guilt can be easily given away—as easily as taking out the garbage. You put it in the can out back, and the next day, it's gone. So simple, and yet I can't help but wonder where it went. If God does as Butcher says, does He collect all the guilt and put it someplace, a cookie jar behind the throne? Or does He recycle it to teach us a lesson?

Isn't it possible that the guilt I'm carrying is actually your guilt—just because giving away my guilt makes me feel better? I can't help but wonder about Cecilia. By me giving away my guilt, does Cecilia feel better? Is she more likely to look at life now like one big fruit basket? I'd like to hope so for her sake, but I kind of doubt it. We can't undo things we have done. Perhaps that is the real lesson in life. We can only attempt to change the subject.

"Spilt milk," Butcher says. "No use worrying about it."

But I do. I can't help thinking that, if I'd been more careful or taken more precautions, the milk would still be in the carton.

"Where do you suppose the milk was before it got into the carton?" Butcher loves saying things like that. He has a way of taking your mind off your troubles and putting them someplace else, a cookie jar perhaps.

He does have a point however. It's not the milk that is the problem, but the carton. The problem with the carton is that the carton is me.

"Wouldn't they have known if your granddad ran over a dog and our pal? I mean he's old, not invisible. Wouldn't someone have noticed and said something?"

He just looked at me with those pitiful eyes of his. His pupils always seemed to be dilated; it made him look inquisitive, even though I know he was not.

"I mean, wouldn't your grandfather have noticed running over a dog and a boy? Wouldn't he have realized something was not quite right?" I couldn't help feeling that Butcher was making all this up. What kind of a person could accept responsibility for the death of a pet and a pal and just show up for supper as if nothing has happened?

"He's like that; you've got to understand. He's old, probably at least fifty. Half the time, he seems not to remember who I am. He's threatened several times to throw my dad out of the house for being an intruder. He keeps asking my mom who that guy is. He keeps telling our dog to go home. Pete just hides under the bed. I think I might try that myself." Butcher seems not to see the relevance of his granddad's intuition.

If life is as Freud said, sons are about replacing their fathers; perhaps fathers are about replacing their sons. It does seem possible.

Butcher tells me Freud is irrelevant. Fathers do not wish to replace their sons but to be their sons. He says his father always wants to know what he's feeling and what he plans on doing with his life and things like that. "Jesus, I'm not quite eleven. How the hell should I know?" Butcher can be quite dramatic when he wishes to be. "So when I don't answer, like I usually don't, he fills in the blanks, like I'm some kind of crossword or something. He keeps trying to tell me that work is a capitalistic plot to keep the masses under the thumb of domination. I could care less. He says education is the only way out. He tells me that it's not that you've got to be smarter than everyone else; what matters is that they believe you are. 'Degrees,' Dad's fond of saying, 'degrees— Masters, PhDs, whatever. Fill your wall with them. Go to school until you can't make it up the steps any longer.' I do finally get it. It's not about education itself—my dad barely got out of high school—it's about the profession of education. Stay in school as long as you can; it beats the hell out of working. Trouble is, I hate school."

Butcher I know doesn't really hate school; he hates the idea of school. But that's a totally different matter altogether. No one likes the idea of school. What's to like? Being pushed around by a bunch of people who don't seem to have a clue as to what it's like to be a student. What the hell happened to these people? How can you forget entirely the most memorable time in your life? If you count the first four years of life as school years, which technically they are if you think about it (walking, talking, and all that), plus the twelve years of school required, plus the four more if you actually can find the money or time to continue on, you've invested a third of your life in schooling, assuming you live into your sixties. You are considered a kid while going to school; therefore, about a third of your life is tied up in being a kid. How do you imagine someone could forget a third of their lives?

Butcher says it's because people are traumatically distorted. Traumatically distorted? I had to ask him what that meant. Well, according to Butcher, it means that, when we are young, events, profound events, have a way of changing our lives and we don't even know it. "Just tell me what it was like the last time you went to the dentist," he said. "See, you don't remember or can't remember. It was so traumatic your mind, without your consent, blocked it out to keep you from going nuts."

"Going nuts?"

"Yes—wacko, off your rocker. Your mind has to do that to keep the rest of you from jumping off the nearest bridge. It's a failsafe mechanism that has developed over time, like evolution, that makes it possible for man to continue killing and maiming and still be able to get up in the morning and eat breakfast. Just think about it."

He may be right. All kinds of things happen to people that they can't remember. Half the stuff I learned in school I've already forgotten, and I can't really say the rest has done me a lot of good. I can't find a way to break the curse. I can't seem to escape this feeling that something terrible is going to happen to me, and I've gotten to the point that I don't care. I know that sounds like I've given up, but it is not that at all. I just don't care. Maybe I've gotten to the point in my life where I see the futility of change and have decided that thing in my head that protects me from unpleasantness by erasing my bad memories, no matter what I change into, will still be futile. I've come to the conclusion that there is no way to outrun a curse.

"When we die, do you think we go to heaven immediately, or do we get to hang around for a few days and see what's happening?" Butcher was continuing to push.

"What?" I asked, trying to figure out what he'd meant.

Butcher moved closer to me, our knees almost touching. "When we die—"

"Yeah, I heard you the first time. What makes you so sure that, when we die, anything happens at all, let alone that we sit around for a few days to check out how everyone is doing? Do you suppose that, after we are dead, we are going to care whether the funeral was nice or that more than two people, relatives probably, came to the service? What are you trying to say?"

Butcher looked hurt. I shouldn't have said that to him. It wasn't his fault. I just get a little edgy sometimes when I can't figure things out. Butcher, although able to dish it out, when challenged, oftentimes can't take it.

This curse thing, I have to admit, has me baffled. When I try and speak to people about it, they look at me like nothing's wrong; it's just the result of an overactive thyroid or something. I tried talking to the priest about it, but all he wanted to know was when my last confession was.

I think talking about death scares people. The more religious people are, the more it seems to scare them. Maybe Butcher and I can talk about these things because we are on the long end of the stick, so to speak. Maybe in ten or fifteen years, when we are old, it will all seem scary to us too. Ten or fifteen years—that seems like such a long time.

"Do you suppose there's a time limit on curses? Could it be like food where, if you don't eat the junk by a specific time, it turns to poison and can kill you?"

Butcher started looking at the ground again and shaking his head. I wondered if we shouldn't go get something to eat. "You hungry?"

Butcher looked up from his ground gazing. "Why not?" Butcher's short attention span, seemingly unbeknownst to him, works to his advantage

We continued to grow physically, Butcher and me. By the following year, we were the same size as Cecilia; by the year after, we were quite a bit taller. Cecilia seemed to have quit growing. It was as if the curse had deprived her of the ability to grow; she'd stopped. Her words whispering in my ear seemed to grow faint after a while, and by the time I had surpassed her in stature, I had not thought of that fateful day in some time.

The anniversary would have, for all practical purposes, gone unnoticed had it not been for Butcher and his news. It wasn't entirely his fault. Truthfully, he had little to do with it. One shouldn't shoot the messenger as they say, but it was he who brought the news. "Cecilia is dead."

I know it's Butcher's way, but he could have broken the news a little more diplomatically in my opinion. I know Cecilia and I were not close; as a matter of fact, we had not spoken since that day. I did, however, feel an unexplainable loss. It was not like finally being rid of a stalker, the grim reaper, which should have given me relief, but it left me feeling tired. That is the only way I can explain it. I felt like someone had let the air out of my tires.

Butcher must have seen the news had affected me because he smiled. He claimed I had no emotion or at least showed none. He claimed I would grow up to be one of those people who talked to themselves all the time and who locked themselves in a closet to cry. I told him I wished he'd go home, that I needed to be alone. His smile grew larger. He knew he was on to something.

"The problem is that curses don't go back in the bottle after the owner has left the premises. You know that, don't you?" Butcher began to weave his new theory, now that the rules had changed.

"What is that supposed to mean? Why can't you talk like everyone else and just say what's on your mind?"

I could see that hurt look again welling up in his eyes.

"Sorry, not your fault; it's just that Cecilia was a, well, she was a classmate of ours. And besides, when someone dies, it's sad, whether they talked to you or not, or even if they put a curse on you. For all we know …" I couldn't go on. I wanted to believe, or at least convince him or me, that there never had been a curse or that, at the last minute, she had taken the curse off. "How'd she die?" I had to know.

His eyes began to lose that glazed look. He didn't answer at first. He seemed to be sizing me up like a prizefighter, waiting to see if he thought I could take the knockout punch.

"You know that long trench coat she always wore, the one with the long belt that was always hanging there like a piece of ravioli? She got off the bus, and it didn't. She got dragged a couple of blocks before anyone noticed the bus was trolling and she was the bait. God what a way to go," Butcher exclaimed, a tone of glee creeping into his voice.

I couldn't help wondering if he was making this all up. "Who told you about Cecilia?"

"Ralph's sister. I ran across her down by the school. She said she'd been getting help, and with any luck, she'd be able to cross the street soon and then we'd be able to see more of one another."

"Why would you want to do that?"

"Do what?" He looked genuinely surprised.

"See more of Ralph's sister?"

"I don't want to see more of her; that was her suggestion. I was telling you that she was the one who told me about Cecilia."

"How'd she find out if she can't leave the block?"

"I don't know, but the next time I see her, I'll be sure to ask."

We do that when we are stressed. "We compensate by being disagreeable, testy, or flippant," as Butcher put it. He likes the word *testy*. He uses it quite a bit, even when it is not appropriate, but he does it anyway. I get the feeling sometimes that he does things just to see if he can get away with them. He likes poking people, kicking them if necessary, to see if he can get them to react. He told me once he thought I was dead. When I asked him what he meant, he just looked at me with those eyes of his until I turned away. He seemed to be able to look inside me and see things even I didn't know were there. He was good at finding cookies.

As it turned out, he was right. Cecilia had died in an accident. The paper didn't go into details. It made it sound like she'd been run over by a bus, which I guess was close enough. People don't like to talk about how children die. It makes them uncomfortable. The paper had a picture of Cecilia, next to who she was survived by—family, grandparents, everyone really—all that stuff. She looked pretty much the same in her picture; I think it was an old one. She had her mouth closed, so you couldn't see she wore braces. That always makes a difference.

Butcher asked if I wanted to go to the funeral. It was at his church, even though Cecilia was Catholic. He said his grandmother worked in the kitchen, and afterward, they'd have lunch. He said we'd get whatever we wanted. Somehow it just didn't seem right, so I stayed home.

Butcher said a lot of people attended ; a lot of kids from school had gone, more than had gone to Ralph's. The schoolThey gave anyone who wanted to go to the funeral the afternoon off. They didn't do that for Ralph's.

Butcher said the coffin had been open when he went with his grandmother. He said Cecilia had looked smaller, kind of like she'd lost weight. She appeared to have been in a fight but otherwise looked the same. He said the chocolate brownies were good, but the Jell-O salad tasted awful. He thought whoever made it had forgotten to put the sugar in it. Her parents closed the casket before the people started coming. They put a picture of her on the lid. He thought it was the same picture that had been in the paper. He said a lot of people cried, and one woman who he thought might have been her mother, fainted and fell on the floor. He said it was best I hadn't gone; I believe he was right. He brought me a paper napkin, a souvenir of the funeral, he said. It was white with purple around the edges and a big purple cross in the middle. Lutherans are funny people sometimes.

It was weird at school for a while after the funeral. Most of the kids knew Cecilia had put a curse on me, even though they never mentioned it. It was funny how just one person could make such a difference. If I remember correctly, Cecilia was never what you'd call sociable. She had a few friends, mostly other girls like herself who seemed to be alone most of the time. It wasn't that they were unpopular; it's just that they weren't popular. I know it's not much of a distinction, but it is a distinction. Her desk now sat empty, like a black hole in the middle of the universe. It was funny how someone who was invisible for the most part now took up so much of the room.

No one talked about her, not even the teacher. I'd watch her eyes move about the room, and then when they came to where Cecilia used to sit, they'd just stop. She seemed to forget the rest of us were there. Her stare was fixed on the empty seat, as though she were waiting patiently for Cecilia to reappear as if nothing had happened. I pictured her more clearly now that she' gone than I could when she was here. I suppose that's not unusual. We all remember things in a different light, a better light than the one they were actually cast under. We tend to fill in the blanks; choose brighter colors; and, when all else fails, invent.

I've tried inventing a new life for myself. So far, it hasn't worked. I've not been able to forget enough of me to make a real difference. One day, while hanging from the parallel bars in the playground by my knees, attempting to do a dismount, I fell. I landed on my head and don't remember much after that. When I came to, I seemed to remember more than I had before I'd fallen. I came to the conclusion that banging my head, even if by accident, didn't seem to have any negative impact on who I was. All I managed to garner from the experience was that falling on one's head hurt like hell.

Butcher asked me just the other day if I'd tried to commit suicide again. I told him that I have never tried to commit suicide; I just can't help thinking about killing myself. He seemed to think that might be my curse—not the actual killing of myself but the having to think about killing myself. It sounded plausible I have to admit, until I remembered that it was Butcher, who had suggested that it might be the dog who was cursed.

I don't feel particularly depressed; nor have I ever. The thought of killing myself doesn't seem at all appealing to me; nor is it revolting. It's just a thought that reoccurs like the sun rising every morning. I sometimes wish it wouldn't, but then, I suppose I'd miss it. The funny thing is I've come to find the notion entertaining. I know it sounds peculiar, or as Butcher says, "sick," but it's really not. It's kind of like watching TV, some bad, some not so bad.

Butcher said that, most often, suicide runs in the family. "It's like being short or fat or stupid. It's not your fault; it just is." I don't know if I can buy that, but it did get me thinking. I've heard that suicide runs in families, like being fat, his words revolved through my head like reruns on TV.

Butcher was good at that; he'd put something in your head he knew you couldn't get out, like the last song you heard on the radio before you went to school.

I asked my mother if anyone in our family had ever committed suicide, probably not a good thing to ask. She looked at me with the most peculiar expression on her face; she put her hand on my forehead and then made me spend the weekend in bed, as if I had pleurisy or something. "Why?" she kept repeating as she led me to my room. "Why would you want to know something like that?"

I tried to convince her I was feeling just fine and the question was just that, a question, But she couldn't get past the idea that she'd come upstairs to find out why I was not ready for school and find me hanging from the closet pole.

My father, although I'm sure he knew what I had asked my mother, never mentioned it. We seemed somehow closer after that. One day, when he was driving me to school, he said in a voice so quiet I had to listen extra hard to hear, "Albert."

"What?"

"Albert," he said.

"What about Albert?" I asked. I could tell from the way he was talking to me that he had something to say but just didn't know how to say it. I tried helping him as much as I dared without frightening him off. I'm quite sure that, if my mother had known what he was up to, it wouldn't have been pleasant for him. My mother was one of those hearts and flowers kinds of people who only see the good in things, even bad things. "Even a mass murderer has a mother," she was fond of saying.

"What about Albert?" I asked. I knew I had an uncle Albert, my grandmother's brother. I had seen pictures of him when he was little and later on, after he'd gotten back from Vietnam. He'd died before I was born, so I'd never gotten to know him. TheyMy parents had never said how he died, and I didn't really care enough to ask, until now that is.

"Albert," my father volunteered, "jumped off a bridge."

"Into the water?" I asked, shocked.

"No," he replied, whispering once again. "He jumped off a bridge onto the train tracks."

"Jesus!" I couldn't help myself.

My father looked at me disapprovingly and then relaxed his face in the forgiving way he had of letting me know profanity was ok under the circumstances.

"Why?" was all I could manage to say.

"Why? Why? Because he was nuts, that's why. When he got back from the war he was not the same guy. He wore brightly colored embroidered shirts with dragons and kangaroos on them and listened for the longest time to nothing but Hawaiian music. Your mother insisted he move in with us until he got settled. I've got to be honest with you, after several months of listening to Hawaiian music, I wanted to kill him myself."

It wasn't like my father to be so forthcoming. I was confused by his story. I can now only believe that he broke the father-son pact about speaking to one another about things that matter because he was genuinely worried about me. God only knows what my mother might have told him. After that, I was never able to look at that picture of my grandmother and Albert standing beside the railroad tracks behind their home without wondering if he hadn't possibly been cursed like me. Maybe he had done something to my grandmother and she'd cursed him. Maybe that is why my mother seems to be so bothered by my questions.

After several weeks of scrutiny on my mother's part, things went back to normal. I no longer made my feelings known or asked any questions, having learned my lesson. Two days in bed is unbearably boring, but also terribly enlightening.

Butcher stopped by on Sunday to see how I was. He told me he'd been by on Saturday, but my mother had refused to let him see me. She'd told him I needed some time to be alone. "So what's the matter with you now?" he asked barely inside the door.

I explained about the question I'd posed to my mother about suicide and the family.

"Jesus, man, don't you know anything? I asked my mother when I was in fourth grade, maybe third, where God came from. She looked a little confused but said nothing. So I said to her that God had to come from someplace, didn't He? God didn't just appear one day as if by magic. He couldn't have just shown up, surprised He was there. He had to have come from someplace."

Butcher got animated when he got excited or involved in something. His arms moved about wildly forming all kinds of shapes in the air, as if he were making balloon animals. His glasses would slide down on his nose, and he'd be looking over the rims at you like some professor. He'd push them up, and they'd slide down. "I learned my lesson then," he said taking his glasses off and pushing them into his shirt pocket. "She hauled me off to Sunday school the next week, and I've been in the custody of Mrs. Johnson ever since. You've got to be extremely careful when you talk to your parents about stuff. They don't seem to be very stable people. Maybe that happens when you get old."

I always appreciated Butcher's observations. He had a way of simplifying the most complex of issues.

"You didn't say anything about the curse did you?" He sat right next to me on the bed, a worried look on his face. "You think she got excited about the suicide thing; bring up the curse, and you'll probably end up in a seminary learning how to perform exorcisms on yourself."

It sounded funny when he said it, but from the look on his face, I could tell he was dead serious, so I just looked at my favorite picture—Willy Mays hitting a ball over the left field fence. That was before he left the New York Giants for San Francisco. Butcher was right of course. Curses are like backward prayers, going down a one-way street the wrong way, or walking up the stairs backwards. Some things are best left unsaid, unless of course you know the person you're talking to understands.

Butcher says there are dreams you run away from and dreams that chase you. I had to think about that for a while. I guess I understand what he was saying. Sometimes we run from things because we are frightened. We don't understand, and therefore, we are afraid. Other times, things chase us. We aren't necessarily afraid of them, but we run because we are being chased. It's a reaction, like sneezing when you're around pepper.

The thing about curses is that, even when you stop running, turn around, and look at them objectively, they still scare the hell out of you. It has nothing to do with fear, that thing that makes the hair on your arms stand up, that lump form in your throat, or even that sadness that brings tears to your eyes is nothing we can explain, it just is.

People often say that life is what you make it. That may be true. Death is what you make it. That may also be true. The difference is that we experience life every minute, hour, and day. As for death, we can only imagine what that might be like. That is why, no matter how bad our lives are, we are still afraid of death, because it could be worse.

Have you ever wondered why those who believe in life after death fear death the most? You'd think that if people really believed in life after death and that is was all that it's cracked up to be, mass suicides perpetrated by those who couldn't wait to get to heaven would be a daily occurrence. They're not because, no matter how devout or learned these people are, the question of uncertainty still remains. It is what Butcher calls the "Souls' Black Hole." Life after death is impossible to prove, and that small matter of doubt, regardless of faith, is what keeps us honest. Sure we can proselytize about eternity, but until the lights actually go out, we can't be sure. Now that very fact should keep me from wanting to end my life, but it has no impact whatsoever.

I do not fear death. It's life that scares me. Even though there is so much I don't know about death, there seems to be a whole lot more I don't know about life. I should say, "I don't understand about life." Butcher and I have discussed this problem quite extensively. For a Lutheran, he seems to have somewhat of a grasp on the spiritual aspects of religion, despite his lack of interests in the saints. He can't quite grasp how a human could perform miracles on God's behalf. I tried explaining it to him, but he doesn't get it. I think that's true of a lot of people. They get stuck on the fact that these people are somehow better than the average person and therefore deserve to be worshiped. No one I know worships saints. They talk to them and ask them for things, but is that really so strange? I hear people all the time talking about how they can't wait to get to heaven to see someone, even a pet.

Saints are no more or less than symbols of qualities that we are supposed to emulate. Think of them as visual aids. One can help you find things, one who makes you want to feed the birds and protect all the animals. There's no end to the number of saints who, if given half the chance, will help us get our act together. Saints are supposed to make us feel better about ourselves. We are supposed to recognize that they were just normal people like ourselves, who excelled at being good in one way or another.

Butcher believes they were normal people who lost their grip on reality. "When is the last time you heard of someone becoming famous for feeding birds or helping people find things? My God, you people are strange."

"I didn't say birds helped people find things, finding a thing was someone else's claim to fame," I had to clarify.

"Gotcha!" he smiled.

He had his mind made up on some things, and there was no changing it. He told me today that Bishop Sheen—he's a famous bishop who had his own TV show—is part of the Catholic strategy for preparing people for the Pope to be president. We both agreed that much too much importance is given to the idea of heaven and hell. They appear like mystical places on a metaphysical map, like Monopoly, but instead of a *Go* and a *Jail* there is a heaven and hell. We are entertained with the notion that heaven is like going to the beach, let's say Honolulu. Hell is like going to New Orleans in October after a hurricane. We can't imagine a heaven or a hell without the physical elements that make them real. When you think of it, unless we have been totally misled, when we die, we leave our bodies behind, right? Without those bodies, the idea of burning in the fires of hell doesn't have the same relevance. Butcher says you can kick a wooden leg all day long, and all that's going to happen is that your toe will get sore or the guy whose leg you're kicking hauls off and slaps the hell out of you. Either way, the only one suffering is you.

I have to agree with him on that. Only two humans supposedly took their bodies with them when they left here—Jesus was one and his mother was the other—and there is still a heated debate about the practicality of either case. What I have a hard time understanding is how people can believe someone took his or her body along to a place where he or she would have no need of one—like taking my swimming trunks to the Antarctic—and yet they can't see the probability of curses. If you are powerful enough to will something to happen, shouldn't you be powerful enough to will that something happens to someone else? If you believe in everlasting life, why is it so difficult to believe in everlasting death, which is what I've got now, thanks to Cecilia? Whether it is real or not is irrelevant. What matters is that I believe it is real, just as you might believe Jesus and Mary boarded a bus for Detroit, avoiding the donkey thing.

When Cecilia first looked at me across the aisle and screamed those immortal words, "Why don't you go kill yourself?" I must admit, I was a bit taken aback. Why would you say that to someone? Why would you say it to someone even if you meant it? I remember only too well this girl of ten—her hair that looked like it had been cut with a bowl on her head, her black-rimmed glasses, and a smile that would make you run for cover. She had knees that were always covered with scabs from her most recent attempt to do something foolish. She was the kind of person who you normally paid little or no attention to. And yet her words burned themselves into my memory with the impact of a falling star.

I now of course realize from watching endless hours of bad television and reading way too many bad books that she was, for all practical purposes, just trying to get my attention. She succeeded. I can't help but wonder how my life would be different if I hadn't heard those fateful words. The reality of life, after all, can be measured in seconds, fractions of seconds. Gold medals won or lost on a fraction of a second. Lives lost in a fraction of a second. The whole idea of seconds gives one the feeling that life is really nothing but a series of random events, seconds really, that add up to nothing more than luck—a second here, a second there, the difference between dying in a car crash and just making the yellow light.

I just missed killing myself once when I was trying desperately to pry open the lid to a box. The large screwdriver I was using slipped and flew past my head. I realized at that moment that I could have become impaled on the blade of the screwdriver, but I wasn't. Luck? Probably. And yet the difference between my lying there with a piece of steal sticking out of my head and me saying to myself, how lucky, was just a few inches, a fraction of a second, the time it takes one to blink. Life seems to be little more than the thickness of dust, and about as stable if you really think about it.

So much of life can be measured in a second. Butcher and I used to play a game, which I know now, after all these years, wasn't a smart game to play. We both liked to shoot bows. We set up a target in his basement, and then after we got pretty good, we went outside. After we got what we called "really good," we'd shoot arrows into the air, straight up. If you waited until just before sunset, you'd see the sun glistening off the feathers. There's a place where the arrow stops its ascent and begins to come down. It's that second I'm talking about. The arrow doesn't just turn around and come down, it pauses, as if it were trying to make up its mind what to do, and then it doesn't turn around and head to earth but falls backward, feathers first. It does that until the weight of the tip causes it to tip downward, and then the race is on.

An object will fall thirty-two feet per second in a vacuum. Not quite as fast here in the real world, but close enough. The arrow starts down, the feathers—blue, red, and orange—glistening in the rays of the sun. It races downward toward the eye of the one looking up at it. That is the time when the game gets dangerous. You think you can judge the descent, but you can't really, because about the time you think you'd better run, the arrow plunges into the soft earth beside you, if you were lucky that is. If you weren't, well then you probably wouldn't notice that you weren't lucky until you found yourself looking down on someone who looked terribly familiar.

I never really thought of the game as anything but a game. Butcher claimed it was my subconscious search for an easy way out—killing myself that is.

I never really saw it that way. When one ends his own life, it should be a bit more deliberate. Accidental anything reeks of sloppiness and chance. I don't believe in either. For those that have not considered death in such premeditated terms, let me assure you that myriad methods to mask a death as accidental do exist. There are, however, ways that mask the accidental and to those who haven't thought about death in these terms, premeditated. However, there is always a chance when one resorts to pills that he or she will be discovered and saved. The same is true with carbon monoxide. There is always that chance ; failing can mean untold hours with a psychiatrist, or worse, a priest. A bullet is irretrievable. Once your finger exerts enough force to release the hammer, there is no reversing the process. The most you could hope for at that point is that you don't end up a vegetable with regrets.

There has to be a time where life, like the arrow, hangs between the here and the hereafter—that fraction of a second where we are dead and don't know it, a feeling, a memory, an insight into the future. It has to be the same feeling one has when walking across the floor. We assume from experience that, with the next step, our foot will land on something solid, and the one after that, and after that. We don't consider the fact that the step we are taking will be our last, and yet, for many, it is.

Butcher doesn't know about the curse. He knows of the curse. We talked about Cecilia and the probability of the curse more times than I care to remember, but he doesn't really believe in curses. I can tell. A curse to most people is the idea of an idea. I know that doesn't make sense unless you think about it. We are all of us products of our ideas, our acceptance of who we think we are. It doesn't matter to us that others don't see us that way, as long as we see ourselves that way. Most of us go through life believing we are someone else. Our perceptions are what keep us alive. If we could truly see ourselves for who we are, we probably wouldn't believe it. I think that's the way Butcher sees it. He believes in the possibility of curses but not the probability.

Butcher believes that I too believe in the possibility, but he cannot see that I am a believer in the probability as well. Just as we don't really see ourselves as others see us, others also don't see us as we actually are. We, therefore, become apparitions of who we want to be and who others want us to be. We, the real we, don't actually exist. We become no more than a contrived image, a figment of imagination, no more real perhaps than the embodiment of a spirit on film. We become actors in our own plays, as well as those of others.

Butcher asked me once if I could really take my own life. I think he was testing me. Sometimes we reach a point when we are so confused by the confusion that we don't or won't trust our own judgment. We no longer know right from wrong, up from down; all we can do is play along, in hopes of finding a clue that will let us escape. He wants to believe that, although the idea of a curse is real, there is still the element of a human being that is capable of releasing oneself from it. It is as though we have the ability to leave the door open, leave the knot loose, and leave the motor running. Even though we are doomed by the inevitable, we still, in some remote part of our beings, are capable of defying the inevitable. Butcher doesn't truly believe in curses any more than I can believe in God and for the same reason. He can't fathom the purpose of life without reward or punishment.

He will not believe that you can have a race without a beginning and an end. He cannot see that the race is what it is all about. It is not the finish that counts but the race itself. We are trained from birth to focus on the end—the end of the week, the end of the month, the end of the school year. It is all about the end. We are not told that what really counts is what leads to the end. The end is nothing; the end is always disappointing because we expect so much more. We delight in the anticipation that is associated with the end, no matter what it is. It is that anticipation that allows us to become the spirit that transcends all reality and, therefore, all unhappiness. We have learned to live in a time and place that exists only in our minds and, therefore, in a place that is incapable of letting us down.

I tried to explain it to Butcher. "Look, we don't know ourselves, others only think they know us, and we are only comfortable when we live in our dreams. If that is the case, how do we know that we are even alive? How do we know that what we believe to be our lives is not just another screenplay that we have devised to entertain ourselves? How do we know that the curse is not really the overshadowing influence of how others see us? How do we know that the others are not actually figments of our imaginations conjured by our minds to keep us out of the reach of reality? We don't. Don't you see that we have no way of proving that we even exist outside of our own dream worlds? If God can exist through faith, why can't we? If we can exist outside of the realm of reality, then is it possible that we are each in our own way, God."

Butcher and I often talk of the spiritual aspects of life, but I don't believe he actually accepts the possibility that God only exists because we do. And me, I can't believe anything else. To believe in a curse, one has to believe that someone or something has the ability to influence not only our actions but also the consequences of those actions. One has to believe that we are capable of distinguishing between reality and dreams; one has to believe in God.

So you see my predicament. I do not believe in God, and yet I believe in the possibility and the probability of a curse. I believe that Cecilia had the power to influence my behavior even after she herself has departed. I believe that, even though I have the ability to change my reality as well as the reality of others, they also have the ability to change mine.

Butcher doesn't believe that a sane person can take his own life.

"Sane?" I've tried to get through to him that none of us is sane, and yet he persists.

He cannot extricate himself from the belief that death by one's own hand is somehow less noble than being consumed by cancer or being run down by a drunk driver. The distinction between dying and the act of dying seems to be his purgatory. He is stuck in limbo, a limbo of his own making. He cannot make the leap from where he is, neither backward into reality nor forward into the dream world we refer to as the future. He is as frozen in time as a woolly mammoth, floundering in his own chilly world, waiting to be discovered by a wandering anthropologist who has nothing better to do. He cannot or will not give me the courtesy of admitting that taking one's own life is no more injurious to one's soul than going mad from fever or being struck in the head by a puck at a hockey game. Butcher is the most stubborn person I believe I know. Perhaps that is why I must forgive him.

I've known Butcher for, I can't remember how long exactly. It seems like forever, but then childhood seems to last forever, until it's over, and that is when I met Butcher. He moved in across the alley from me. He was taller than I was, I assumed older at first. He had short hair that stood up as though it were itself frozen in time. He had round eyes, large round eyes that seemed to look right inside of you. You couldn't tell a lie to Butcher; at least I couldn't. I had the feeling he would know the truth, and besides, what would be the point? I was ten. What would I have to lie about? What I had, he could see. He had thin arms; I remember that. Isn't it funny the things you remember about someone—the things that make an impression. His arms seemed to be so thin it was hard to believe anything was beneath the skin but air. I liked him immediately.

He had a brother, who I know now was, for all practical purposes, dead. He walked around like everyone else and talked like everyone else, but there was something about him that made me think of him as dead. It wasn't that I am clairvoyant or anything like that; it was just that he made me shiver to look at him. He was several years older than Butcher. He had black hair, the blackest I'd ever seen; it was almost purple it was so black. He combed it back leaving his forehead naked, like a vacant billboard along the highway. He had dark eyebrows that seemed to make his eyes look foreboding, like those of a fortuneteller. He reminded me of James Dean; James Dean before he died in that auto accident.

Butcher lived with his brother and parents in a duplex. They lived downstairs; I can't remember ever seeing anyone who lived upstairs. Butcher was nothing like his brother. I guess that is not all that unusual; a lot of siblings are not alike. His brother however was more different than that. Something about the look in his eyes made me want to make the sign of the cross every time I saw him. It wasn't because I was afraid of him but because he gave me the same feeling I got when the lights would go out and the shirt on the back of my chair in my room would turn into a creature of the night. Unlike most creatures that would disappear when you pulled the covers over your head, Butcher's brother would only become more menacing if you didn't look at him.

Butcher's brother—I think his name was Dick; I never thought of him in any other way than Butcher's brother—died when he was twenty years old in the war. Before he moved, Butcher came over and we sat on the grass by our garage and told me the police had taken his brother to jail for breaking all the windows in the school across from their house. He apparently had put his fist through many of the windows on the first floor of the building and then gone home. The police followed the trail of blood to his house.

I don't look at the obituary columns in the paper. I was sitting in the dentist's office, waiting as you always do, when I saw the picture of this guy in the paper that looked so familiar. The paper was just sitting next to me on the red plastic cushions. I looked at it for several minutes feeling uncomfortable, as if I were looking at a particularly gruesome accident. It was the eyes, I guess, that caused me to read the words below the picture. He had died in Vietnam, survived by his parents. He had the same look that had caused me to make the sign of the cross when I'd see him. I found my hand acting of its own volition, touching my head and my shoulders involuntarily, as though my hand belonged to someone else.

Butcher's brother went to what Butcher referred to as reform school after breaking the windows in the school. I never saw him again. Butcher was not the same after that. He seemed more withdrawn, more forgetful, more Lutheran. He began to pick fights over the most trivial things. He told me for the umpteenth time that, if Kennedy were elected president, the Pope would be running the country. I think he came to believe it. I told him I thought he was full of crap, and he hit me. We didn't speak for some time after that. But then, like a thunderstorm, our estrangement was over, and things went back to normal for a while. I think he was just upset.

It's funny now that I look back on things that I can still remember the feeling I'd get when looking at his brother—the feeling that he was already dead and didn't know it. I tried to tell Butcher one time about my premonition, but he wouldn't listen. He only laughed, his nervous laugh, the one he used when he didn't know what else to do, and then punched me in the arm. I had a black and blue mark for a couple of weeks where he punched me. I didn't talk to him about his brother after that, even though I knew he was already dead.

It was a funny thing; Butcher died before his brother. I didn't see that coming however. Maybe it was because Butcher and I were too close. Often, we can't see things that are too close to us. We need to get back so the picture comes into focus. I didn't get far enough back until it was too late of course, but then isn't that the way it goes? Butcher fell under the wheels of a train car. I went to the place in the yards where he was killed after I found out. I'm pretty sure he was run over by a Northern Pacific car. At least one of the kids that was with him said it was a Northern Pacific car. One was sitting there when I went to see; it was a rather old, faded red color with broken slats on its side. I looked for signs of blood on its steel wheels but couldn't find any, but then it had rained several times since the accident. They said he was trying to jump onto the moving car when he slipped under the wheels.

They said he died while his friend was off trying to get help. He bled to death after the steel wheels amputated his legs. I couldn't help but wonder what it was like lying there with no legs; I assume he knew his legs were gone, waiting. I wondered often if he knew he was going to die or thought maybe he'd be okay. I often wondered how long he lived after the kid who was with him had gone for help. Not long I'm guessing; I bet he died soon afterward.

Butcher He'd wanted me to go with him that day. I was always both sad and happy I didn't go; I couldn't make myself go. I made up a story so he wouldn't get mad. I think I told him I had to go with my parents someplace. It was a lie, but I just had this terrible feeling that I shouldn't go. I should have warned him. I guess I didn't because he'd been acting so weird. I should have told him that, when I looked into his eyes, I saw his brother looking back at me.

You hear stories of people who have the ability to foresee events. I'm not one of them. I don't see what's about to happen. I didn't see Butcher lying under the tracks, his severed legs on the other side of the rail from his torso. I didn't see him breathe his last breath, say his last prayer. I did feel the life leave his body as he turned from me, disappointed that I wouldn't go with him. His eyes turned to pools of black water that no longer reflected the light of day. I didn't see him die, but I felt him die. I think in some ways that was worse.

When you see something happen, it becomes a negative that your memory returns to for clarification. When you feel something happen, your memory has no clarity but is free to roam about your mind looking for details to justify the consequences of that feeling. Your mind pictures various scenarios in an attempt to reconcile the event and the outcome. It is human nature to look for reasons why things happen. We need to know so that we may put it aside and move on. It is an opportunity to prove to ourselves that we were ultimately not responsible for the tragedy. It is our way of absolving ourselves from guilt.

I didn't go to Butcher's funeral. It wasn't because I felt a sense of guilt or felt in anyway responsible for his death. I had not placed a curse on him or wished him ill in anyway. I had merely been witness to his passing. Sometimes, when you know something is going to happen, you prepare for the outcome. It is really no different than letting a plate fall from your hand. You know the plate will shatter when it hits the floor. You are not surprised by the outcome. You may be angry but not at the plate, not at the floor. Perhaps you're angry at yourself for being careless, but not for the outcome. When you know the outcome, you accept it even if you do not accept the reason for it happening. I knew Butcher was going to die. I saw it in his eyes just as I had seen his brother's death in his eyes. There was nothing to be surprised about; therefore, there was nothing to be sad about, for I had no way of changing the outcome.

What I miss most about Butcher is that I no longer have anyone to talk to. Despite him being a Lutheran and having the limited vision that goes with it, he did listen. I guess that is what I miss most of all—someone who listens. He went with me to confession a couple of times, just to see what it was like. I believe he picked up some valuable pointers. At the very least, he stopped bringing up the matter of the Pope running the country. He may have just decided that he would do that as his penance rather than say all the *Hail Marys* and *Our Fathers* that were traditionally handed out. He never said, and I never asked.

I had a dream about Cecilia last night. It wasn't a nightmare or anything like that. I rarely have nightmares, or if I do, I don't remember them. I never remember any of my dreams, which is why this particular dream seemed so memorable. Cecilia was dressed in her First Communion dress, white. She wore white shoes, stockings, and hat. I think she even had a small, white handbag. She was standing on the steps of the church, a large red brick edifice whose spire poked its shimmering cross at the heavens. She had a tight-lipped smile on her face; her unblinking eyes looked into mine as though searching for understanding. She stood statuesque, a glass beaded rosary dangling from her folded hands, its green glass matching her eye color exactly.

As others, children, parents, and other first communion participants dressed in white paraded around her, she did not move; her non-blinking eyes fixed on me. It was like looking at a photograph where the main subject remained still while the others in the photo moved. And then the others in the photo were gone. She stood alone on the concrete steps leading to the massive wooden doors; the only sound was the ringing of the bells in the tower, at first barely audible and then becoming louder. They were playing the tune of *Happy Birthday*; her shoes had changed from the shiny white of patent leather to black. I could see myself reflected in them. I was no longer a boy but appeared as I do now.

I looked at my hands, and I did not recognize them. They were rough and callused. I looked back at her, and she was now standing next to someone. At first, I didn't recognize the figure. He was dressed in white—white shirt, white suit coat, white pants—and a sky blue tie. He was bare footed; his hands were sandwiched together in prayer, his face was down, and his hair meticulously combed. He raised his face slowly toward mine, and I could see it was Butcher. He smiled at me; he seemed so happy and proud. I watched his hands separate, him reaching into his pocket and pulling from it a spike—a railroad spike, gold. He held it out to me.

As I reached for the spike, I noticed that Cecilia had placed her veiled head close to his and appeared to be whispering in his ear. She turned, and they both smiled at me, their lips tight and their eyes non-blinking. I closed my eyes momentarily, listening to the bells. I wondered whose birthday it was. My head fell backward as if too heavy to control. My eyes opened, and I could see the bells in the tower moving back and forth rhythmically. I forced myself to look down, and Cecilia was there alone once more. A pair of legs clad in white trousers, feet bare, disappeared behind the large doors, the heavy thud of the wood against the jamb as it closed silencing the bells.

Cecilia had not moved. Her eyes, bright green, looked at me as though I was invisible. She looked past me to the street, where the worshipers now hurriedly made their way home. I tried to speak, to ask her what she wanted of me; no words would come. She raised her arm, pointing a finger at me and then beckoning me to come toward her. I tried to move, but my feet would not budge. It was as if they were stuck to the concrete of the walk. I looked down and could see the concrete had turned molten; my shoes had disappeared into its gray mass. I continued to sink, the gray mud now to my knees. I tried to pull my feet free but began to sink more quickly. I stretched my arms before me as the mud rose to cover my chest. A candy bar floated effortlessly out of my reach. I looked at Cecilia, my screams still silent, she still pointing as if accepting my quandary.

The doors of the church opened with a screeching noise, the sound hanging like a memory. The torso of Butcher came floating through the door and down toward me, knocking Cecilia to the steps. Butcher floated toward me, closer, still closer. The gray mud was now covering my mouth; my head tilted back to keep my nose free and my eyes looking up at him. He reached for me; taking my hand in his cold fingers, he began to pull. I did not move. He turned toward Cecilia. I could see his mouth move, but no sound escaped. She looked at him, puzzled, her eyes wide, her brow raised as if she didn't understand. She reluctantly stood and walked toward us, placing her arms around Butcher's waist.

I found myself staring at the ceiling. I was wet with fever, cold, shaking as though I'd been pulled from an ice-covered pond. I could hear my mother in the kitchen preparing breakfast. I lay for a long while remembering the events of the dream, everything so clear, so unmistakably real. As I thought back over the events at the church, I couldn't help wonder why she'd done it—why she'd helped. And then it became clear to me; I would have defied the curse. I needed to find death at my own hand, not the hand of another. She was reminding me that it was my curse, my responsibility to live up to it, to fulfill its intent. She was challenging me to honor my commitment.

I had talked with Butcher once about that very thing, seated in his backyard next to the pole surrounded by hollyhocks, their flowers pink, red, and feeling like paper. Their stamens sparkled with an iridescent yellow that seemed to fall like golden flakes from tiny threadlike hairs. Their leaves a bitter green, felt like Velcro to the touch; their stalks tall, six feet or more, were hollow like an old oak and brittle like bones. "You have a responsibility to honor her curse? Are you nuts?" He was practically yelling. "It's like she's asking you to shoot yourself and then wanting to borrow some money from you to buy the bullet."

He didn't seem to understand. I did. I understood what she was telling me. It was like Christmas or birthdays, a gift. When you receive a gift, you also receive the responsibility that goes with that gift. You are obligated if you will, to be grateful, or at least thankful. You are obligated, even if in a small way, to be appreciative. We have an obligation to respect the wishes of the one giving the gift. Whether you believe the curse was really a gift or whether you wish to assume the responsibility for it has to be left up to each individual.

Butcher would not understand. He would get like that sometimes. He would not listen, no matter how the facts were given proving your assertions. He refused to see the connections between people. He refused to see the distinction between want and need, poor and rich, up and down; he could not understand that distinctions mattered.

"It's all bullshit. It's just another way people manipulate words to make themselves feel better about kicking the shit out of someone, figuratively speaking that is. Want and need are the same if you're on the desert and the sun is beating down on you and water is your only hope. Poor and rich are meaningless words when compared to something as consequential as values. And up and down basically depend on which way you are facing. They are just words. It is only people who do not know how they feel about something who resort to using these words. It makes them feel comfortable. It's like puppies and babies; people hide behind them. No one conjures up the sight of a half-starved kid when someone says baby; they picture some chubby little kid with a smile on his face."

I had to admit he had a point, but I couldn't escape the importance of distinction. It may have been my grandmother's fault, or maybe not.

You know how it is when people say something that may seem totally trivial and irrelevant to them but to you it is devastating. The speaker may have meant no harm or even considered what he was saying as being of any significant importance to you. It's nothing, I can assure you, like the complete frontal attack of words like, "Go kill yourself." It can be and often is something much more subtle. Come to think of it, it wasn't even my grandmother who said it to me. Don't get me wrong; she said a lot of things to me that would have made paint flake, but on this occasion, it wasn't her. It was my cousin's grandmother, my uncle's mother, my aunt's mother-in-law.

She was about eighty then, maybe older. She sat mostly in an old rocking chair that squeaked over her raspy breathing. She had white hair, which she braided and kept in a knot on top her head. She wore wire-rimmed glasses, bifocals, which when she looked down on you made her look like she had two sets of eyes. She wore heavy nylon stockings, the kind you use to hold your tomato plants to the stake in late summer. She smelled of sulfur, or urine, or possibly both. She enjoyed patting children on the head, pinching their cheeks, and placing her head just a few inches from your face when asking "What was your name?"

I tried to avoid her whenever possible. Her breath smelled stale, as though it had been in her for much longer than it should have been. I'd usually look through the storm door to see if she was in the living room. Most of the time, she stayed in her bedroom, but you just never knew. This particular day, I'd been in a hurry, had to get to the bathroom or something, and I hadn't made it halfway across the living room toward the hall when her bony hand shot out from under her afghan and grabbed me. She pulled me toward her, impaling me on her sharp knees. She then pushed me away as if to get a better look at me, squinting. "You're a good boy," she said, "a good boy—not very good-looking, but a good boy."

I always wanted to believe she'd meant no harm, but at the age of eleven, when nothing fits but your socks, her assessment of my looks was a devastating blow. My self-esteem deflated like an escaped balloon, darting about the room frantically. It was as if she'd punched me in the stomach. She died shortly after that. Her demise also burdened my young soul, if you must know. When you wish someone dead, you don't really mean it—or at least that is what you tell yourself.

Standing there by the coffin looking down on her rouged face, I did, however, feel a sense of retribution that I had not felt before. I gained a sense of power that helped partially inflate my balloon. I also, while looking down at her skin shrink over her bones, couldn't help but be honest with not only myself but with her. I had wished her dead, and I'd meant it. I think she took it pretty well when I confessed. I don't think she held it against me. I didn't put a curse on her or anything like that. I simply wished her dead. The rest was up to nature, not me or her. As far as I was concerned, there was no obligation on her part, a fine distinction you may argue, and I would most certainly agree. I thought I saw her blink, but I realized later it was probably only grief, on my part that is.

I do not blame myself for the old lady's death any more than I blame myself for Cecilia's death. As a matter of fact, I believe that, in a way, Cecilia caused her own death. She didn't take her own life and wasn't probably even aware she'd played a hand in her own death, but I believe she did. She was distracted by the responsibility of the curse as much as I was. Most people assume curses are a one-way deal. I give it to you, and you have it—like tag. It doesn't work that way. The connection, the one Butcher failed to admit he saw, does exist.

To explain it in Butcher's words, "You have an itch. You have a scratcher. Together, you have relief. By itself, you have discomfort on the one hand and something with nothing to do on the other." It's the connection between the "doer and the do-ee," as Butcher would say. Most people automatically jump to the conclusion that it is a symbiotic relationship. It is not. One is not sustained by the other; if anything, quite the opposite is true. If I had to describe the connection, I would have to describe it as a complimentary relationship. That's not to say each party makes the other look better; it simply means that each party helps the other understand the relevance of the individual parts. It's kind of like the music in a movie. It sets the mood, it quickens the pace, and it makes you feel good about jumping off the cliff.

I can honestly say I do not feel guilty about Cecilia, even though I know I could have prevented her death. I even tried once to steal that damned canvas belt that hung like a snake's tongue from the front of her coat. Had I succeeded, I would have actually saved her life no doubt, and I believe that would have given me some would have given me relief from the guilt.

I wish I could say I got over my punch in the stomach, but I never did. I think times in your life have a certain impact so profound we never totally recover from them. A bad report card, a failed promise, being deceived or, worse, lied to—these things all push us a little closer to the dark side of the moon. I know it isn't quite as dramatic as that, but when you begin to add up the damage over a few years, it definitely takes its toll.

I told Butcher about the old lady. All he could say was, "So you killed her. So what? She was old, probably going to die anyway. You did her a big favor if you ask me." Sometimes he could be just the one you needed to talk to. He settled my nerves and made me feel somehow forgiven.

Since Butcher's death, I haven't really had anyone to talk to. It has been a long time since I've opened my notebook. The notebook was just one of those binder types that you can get anywhere really. It was blue. I remember when we went to pick it out. He wanted the green one; I wanted the blue. It was my curse, so I got the blue. Butcher always had the cover folded back on itself so you couldn't tell what color it was. I know he did that on purpose. We got the book so we could keep track of our plans, my plans really. He was supposed to help me think of ways to kill myself. Each time we'd come up with an idea, we'd write it in the book. Every week, we'd go back over the ideas and discuss them in detail. Analyze I guess would be a better word. We'd discuss not only the means of death but also the probability of success. We had even worked in a pain threshold, the amount of time it would take to die, and the cost of cleanup. Cleanup is always part of the equation. Some plans are too costly for survivors. Killing yourself is one thing; bankrupting the family is something else. Of all the plans, I never once contemplated throwing myself under a train. Even though I don't believe Butcher would have approved, I wrote it in the notebook anyway- *chance of success—100 percent.*

I met someone today. She is quite nice. I don't know how we got to talking about suicide or curses, but I found her to be quite understanding and knowledgeable about the subjects. I met her on the Ford Bridge; it separates Minneapolis from St. Paul, not much of a distinction really. She was standing by the railing looking down into the muddy water. I enjoy doing that myself. I don't know what made me talk to her; I normally don't talk to strangers. I don't even remember saying it or thinking it; it just kind of jumped out like I'd been saving it for a long time. It was like one of those things you'd wished you'd said, but you didn't think of it until it was too late. I said, "Nice day for a jump."

She said, "I believe you're right. A might windy perhaps, but then, if you calculated, you probably would miss the concrete pier."

We both smiled at each other, as though we both got the joke, and then we went and had coffee.

Her name is Stranger, or that is what she told me. I don't think it's her real name, but then does it matter? She paid for the coffee. She wasn't pretty or ugly, she was just a girl, and she didn't remind me at all of Cecilia. Sometimes when you think a lot about someone, everything you see or touch reminds you in one way or the other of them. She didn't remind me of Butcher either; I liked her from the start. She said she was an Indian. I didn't know what to make of that. I'm no good with nationalities, probably because my heritage is so mixed. I didn't know whether she meant Indian like from India or Indian like from North Minneapolis. It didn't really matter to me, but I believe it did to her because she mentioned it. All one can do at that point is smile and say, "That's nice."

I hate that phrase, so I just smiled, a little.

She asked me if I knew what my name meant. I had to admit I had never really thought of it.

"Well, you should," she said emphatically, as though it would change my life. She said her name meant *unknown origin*. I kept wondering why she'd been standing on the bridge and forgot to ask her anymore about her name. It didn't seem to bother her. She went right on explaining as though I'd asked. I like a person like that. They believe so strongly in what they are doing that they don't really need an audience. I appreciated that, and I told her so. We decided to go out.. We would meet on the bridge at sunset. I planned to tell her of the curse.

I usually don't tell people I've just met about the curse because it tends to shorten the friendship if there were to be one. But on the other hand, I feel I've wasted too much time on people who only disappoint me. I have decided that, if I am to be left alone, I'd rather it be done quickly. I'm not much of one for dressing up. I never could get attached to the notion that clothes make the man.

I did, however, put on clean socks and managed to get to the bridge on time. She was already waiting, a good sign; most of the time my clandestine meetings never materialize. People are hard to get to know.

She turned as I approached and smiled. Her teeth were bright against her dark skin, her large eyes pregnant with tears; I hoped she was happy to see me. "They call me Angel," she said, taking my hand and holding it to her cheek. She closed her eyes and listened. "Your heart is beating fast," she mimed over the sounds of the river, as though she were afraid it might hear. "Are you frightened?" She didn't wait for an answer but began to walk toward the setting sun still holding my hand. "My name is—" She jerked me into a fast walk and then a run. "We must get off the bridge," she whispered, looking down into the murky, brown water. My hand began to hurt she squeezed so hard; I followed in hopes she'd let go when we reached the other side. She did.

"I had a premonition," she said, loosening her grip. "I can't explain it; I just knew we had to get off the bridge."

"I had the same feeling," I said.

She smiled at me and once again and placed my hand in hers.

"Except my feeling wanted me to go the other way to get off the bridge."

"Closer?" she said, squeezing my hand once more.

"Closer," I said, a tear running down my cheek. She smiled and squeezed harder.

"To the restaurant," I continued.

She relaxed her grip. "What kind of food do you like?" I asked, putting my hands in my pockets.

"Soup," she said, her eyes becoming slits as she scrutinized my intentions.

"Yes, soup, the perfect meal," I said, remembering what Butcher had told me about the curative powers of soup.

"Then soup it is," she said, sliding her arm through mine.

Sometimes, you meet someone and you feel you've known herthem forever, and other times, you've known someone forever and you find you don't know them at all. I don't quite know how to explain it, but she was both at the same time. She made me comfortable and uneasy all in the space of a couple of words.

"Split pea or vegetable?" the waitress wanted to know. She was a small woman, maybe twenty, pretty hair and bright sky eyes. She smiled at me, waiting, her pencil poised above her pad as though hanging on my every word.

Before I could answer, Stranger blurted out, "Ham and cheese, and make it quick."

The young woman looked startled and then began to write furiously on her pad. I watched her pencil move cautiously across the small, blue, lined pages, gaining speed as she progressed toward the bottom. She stopped abruptly and sat down on the red artificial plastic of the cushion across from us. She began to writing furiously.

I watched as she filled one page after the next and then quit as quickly as she'd begun.

Stranger had paid no attention. She'd dumped the contents of the saltshaker onto the Formica tabletop and had begun to draw designs in the bed of salt. She reached several times for the pepper shaker but, thinking better of it, stopped each time, content to draw on the bed of white.

"I'm sorry," said the young woman across from us. "What was that you said?" Not waiting for a response, she added, "I'm a songwriter, and sometimes when I get an idea, I have to write it down or I forget. I didn't mean to be rude, sorry." She tore the dozen or so blue, lined pages from the pad and stuffed them into her breast pocket.

Stranger busied herself with the intricacies of salt painting, seemingly lost in her art. I began again, "I'll have a …"

And the young woman with the nice hair began to scribble once more on her pad. When she'd finished, she jumped to her feet and headed for the rear of the room, stopping at the kitchen to pull her coat from a hook, and proceeded down the aisle and out the door into the alley.

Stranger picked up the pepper shaker and placed it in the middle of her intricate design, which reminded me of the signs that floated around the heads of cartoon characters as they were pummeled by falling rocks or being run over by locomotives. Stranger smiled awkwardly at her creation and then, wiping her creation onto the floor with the back of her hand, said softly, as though asking me to go home with her, "What's for supper?"

I could hear the humming coming from the alley. The door had lodged open when the waitress burst through causing it to stick in the open position. I watched her pace back and forth as though on a parade field on the Fourth of July, humming more loudly with each passing.

"What do you think about Chinese?" I offered.

"I'm not prejudiced if that's what you mean."

"No, I mean do you like Chinese food?"

"No." She was abrupt. "I don't like the stuff that makes everything stick to everything else."

"MSG?" I suggested.

"I don't know what you call it, but it makes me feel like I've eaten a barrel of glue."

"What kind of soup did you say you liked?" I said as I watched the waitress march, now stiff legged back and forth before the door, holding a comb beneath her nose.

"Chicken noodle," she offered.

"Make that two," I yelled at the rear door.

The waitress smiled and gave me the okay sign. We never saw her again.

We waited for what I considered to be an appropriate amount of time. The green tea in our Styrofoam cups grew cold; leaving their sides a stained algae green. Undissolved sugar was piled at the bottom of the cup like driven snow. Stranger began to unscrew the top of the salt dispenser once more.

"What do you say we get out of here?" I don't normally like to take control of the situation. I found it makes life more complicated. Once you've declared your intentions, you become pushy, manipulative, or overbearing, depending upon who you are with. Perhaps it was the lime green stain escaping into the pores of the cup that caused me to be more decisive than usual. Once you take a stand or declare your intent, it is as if you'd drawn a line in the sand. It fuels tension and creates discord; you are on one side or the other.

"Sure, why not," was all she said, returning the salt container to its place in the small rack and slipping its chrome, hole-filled lid into her pocket. "This will come in handy," she said, sliding from the booth.

We walked to the door, she carrying her half empty cup, lime green leaves floating ominously on the remaining liquid. As I pushed the door open, the bells attached to its top rang their displeasure. I held the door for Stranger as she made her way onto the sidewalk balancing her Styrofoam memento in one hand while searching her pocket for her newfound talisman.

A boy of about twelve, upon hearing the bells signaling our escape, emerged from the kitchen doorway carrying a tray with two larger versions of Styrofoam cups, each with a plastic spoon handle protruding from its open top. He stopped as he saw me standing in the doorway; a look of disappointment formed on his face. He looked exactly like Butcher; he too was barefoot.

I let the door fall back into place, the attached bells jingling awkwardly as we walked along the bank of windows painted with the lavish colors of a high school homecoming. The boy stood motionless, following our progress with fixed eyes. Stranger pulled the talisman from her pocket; briskly polished it on her shirt; and then stopped, staring through the window at the twelve-year-old statue. She lifted her prize to the window and then waved.

I could see the boy's lips begin to move. I heard no sound but could make out the words formed by his mouth. "What about the soup?"

Stranger placed the chrome talisman in my hand and then wrapped the fingers of her hand around mine, pulling me down the street toward the river. I was in the midst of my one-handed shrug by the time the tray hit the floor.

We walked for some time, neither of us speaking; I slipped the shaker lid back into her pocket. She sipped from her cup, periodically causing disruption in our otherwise choreographed gait. She had long legs, and her strides were deliberate, as if she were intent upon reaching a place. I had difficulty keeping up with her, having done no real walking or exercising, well, ever. My heart was pounding, and I found myself being grateful that she carried the tea. I had the overpowering feeling that, somehow, she was saving my life, if only in an indirect way.

As we approached the place on the bridge where we'd met just a short time before, she abruptly stopped. I being consumed with the challenge of keeping up with her and not expecting the sudden change, managed to collide with her, our shoulders coming in contact with one another like football players. In an attempt to keep her balance, she let go of the cup. Its contents spilled onto the stained concrete, followed a crack toward the rail, and then dripped over the side a drop at a time, mixing with the waters below.

"A sign," she said, watching the liquid flow to its final destination. "You do believe in signs, don't you?"

"What do you mean by a sign?" I managed, feeling slightly embarrassed by my clumsiness.

"You do believe there are those we do not see who tell us things if we will only listen?" She studied me for what seemed a long while, scrutinizing my face through eyes that looked out on me from slits on either side of her wrinkled nose and furrowed brow.

I guessed I believe in signs. I had never really thought much about it. I know people attribute all manner of luck or misfortune to physical monuments. Rocks, trees, the sun and moon, bottle caps—all play critical roles in the futures of some people. And then I realized that I had no idea which sign she was referring to. Was it the lime green tea now mixing with the contents of the mighty river or the fact that I had nearly ran her over? Would she see my contact with her as a sign of intimacy or perhaps an attempt to push her over the edge?

"Most white people only believe in one sign, the sign of the cross. They are so unimaginative." She walked over to the railing and, leaning over, watched as the remaining drops of algae-colored water disappeared into the swirling brown waters below.

I wasn't insulted by her remarks. I could have been, or possibly I should have been, but then she was entitled to her opinion, Indian or not. I stood beside her, leaning over the railing as well and watching the water below. A barge moved slowly from beneath the bridge being pushed by a tugboat. The words *Drunken Mermaid* were printed on the roof of the cabin above a picture of a woman with large breasts and a fish tail, possibly a walleye's. It occurred to me that I had a heritage, I had an oral history, and I had a culture. Because it was not as old as hers did not make it any less meaningful.

My family too had suffered at the hands of the New Republic; our language, our customs had all been blurred in an attempt to homogenize our people. Our language had been forbidden. Our customs had been outlawed by those who saw distinction as being detrimental to the blandness inherent in a controlled society. My people, my tribe had been sold the prospect of prosperity for the small sum of our heritage. We'd bought it gladly, never questioning the fact that the promise of prosperity had the same value as glass beads. We too were forced onto reservations, some rural, some urban, to work the fields and factories to build a new society based on the principles of freedom and justice for all those who could afford it.

As I leaned over the railing looking at the barge progressing upriver, I could feel the anger build in me, My heart beating faster and my temperature began to rise. The sign of the cross, indeed!

I looked at her next to me, her black hair flowing away from her head in the breeze. She looked quite beautiful. *What about lutefisk, potato dumplings, sauerkraut, boiled ham and cabbage? What about pierogies?* I wanted to scream, but I didn't. I wasn't raised that way, so I said nothing. "What do you feel like doing now that we've covered the barge traffic and soon it will be too dark to see the river? Any thoughts? Any signs?"

She took the talisman from her pocket. She pulled a handkerchief from the inside of her pocket and meticulously wiped the chrome surface, being careful not to touch it with her skin. "Fingerprints," she mumbled. And then, holding the hole-filled cover in her outstretched, handkerchief-covered hand, she let both the handkerchief and the cover drop. The handkerchief was blown immediately into the air and appeared to be chasing the barge. The chrome moon fell slowly, turning over and over as though it had no idea what to do. I lost sight of it before it hit the water.

"They'll never be able to pin that on me," she said, taking my hand once again in hers and pulling me toward the far end of the bridge. "Bastards!"

We spent the night on the screened-in porch of the duplex where she lived with her sister and her sister's boyfriend. I slept, or should say I attempted to sleep, on a glider swing that squeaked with every breath. She had curled up in an old beanbag chair that oozed pellets onto the concrete floor. Moths fluttered about the outside light, and an occasional bat would swoop past the door, leaving only a shadow as a reminder of its presence.

I had just found sleep when a taxi pulled up outside. The slamming of doors and the voices drove sleep into the shadows. I slept no more that night; nor did Stranger. We pretended to sleep as the cab's occupants stumbled onto the porch, the woman tripping, putting her hand through the rusty screen as though it were but an illusion. "Shit, shit, shit, shit."

And then they were gone as quickly as they'd come. I watched as the illuminated sign on top of the cab disappeared around the corner.

"You awake?" she asked, getting up and sitting next to me on the rusty metal swing.

A black hole, a wonderful period during any given night when time ceases to exist. It is a time where sleep will not come because it refuses to, a time when your mind and body seem to separate into the physical and the spiritual, a time where everything looks as though it were dipped in fog. Your words are more profound, the truth more visible, lies believable, and love more possible. I love that time of night. I feel like I can take my head off and put it on the shelf and somehow think more clearly. All of my senses are heightened. Popcorn brings tears to your eyes, and chocolate makes your body shudder like an addict's. It is the time when words are either too much or too little, where sometimes, words are not necessary at all. A look, just a simple look will convey all that needs to be said and understood. It was like that on the porch that night, sitting on the rusted metal glider waiting for the first rays of morning to break the spell.

Stranger had been raised by wolves—not the conventional or traditional wolves one imagines but wolves nevertheless; when she was three, her mother and father died in an ice fishing accident on some obscure northern lake. They apparently fell asleep with the stove on. "It was not carbon monoxide poisoning," she said emphatically. "Everyone assumes when I tell them this story that they died of carbon monoxide because it is how most people die. They did not. The stove caused the ice to melt, and the whole thing slipped into the icy water, where they were trapped in the shack and drowned." She was then placed in a series of foster homes, where she claimed her new parents did everything possible to make her into an average, all-American, white kid. She claimed one family even dyed her hair blond. She ran away. When she was sixteen, she ran away to live with her sister, the two of them had been together ever since.

The night was warm. The crickets sang slightly off key as we rocked back and forth to the grating sound of metal on metal.

"Do you believe in curses?" There is no easy way to lead into a question like that, and sometimes the shock that comes with the suddenness pulls the truth from someone before they've had a chance to devise a plan to escape into a noncommittal realm of aloofness.

Stranger seemed to be unscathed by my question. I watched her face, bathed in the yellow glow of the streetlamp. She didn't even blink. I put my arm on the cold back of the swing and waited. I could tell she was contemplating an answer by the increased speed of our rocking. She finally stiffened as though struck by an electrical impulse, leaned her head back onto my arm, nestled her shoulder against my chest, and sighed.

She smelled good, baby powder good. Her straight black hair spread across my shirt like an expensive scarf. I closed my eyes and felt her words vibrate through me. "I've been cursed my whole life. Do you think being an Indian is easy? Our people believe we were all cursed when the morons on the East Coast let Columbus live. It has been our curse to be a good and noble people. And look what it has gotten us."

"No, that's not what I mean," I said. "I don't mean cursed as in bad luck or poor timing or being in the wrong place at the wrong time. I mean cursed—cursed like when someone yells in your face that she hopes you die or rot in hell or that you go kill yourself, that kind of curse. I'm talking about when some power that you cannot see or touch or possibly doesn't even exist can cause you to do something you may wish not to. Do you understand what I'm saying?"

She did not answer. I sat quietly listening to her breath lap against me like waves on the shore. I felt my eyes close. I had a sensation I was falling, deeper and deeper into the darkness, blacker than the bottom of a well. I was floating, drifting downward like a feather. I felt the light disappearing above me, and then I saw Cecilia's face. She was wearing her white dress and had the veil of her white hat pulled over her face. She leaned closer to me, and I could see through the fine, white mesh that her skin was raw and her eyes were black. Her brown canvas belt was wrapped around her neck like a tie, and she was trying to speak, but no sounds came. I leaned closer and could hear a voice. It didn't sound like her voice. It was deep and scratchy, the sound of streptococcus. The words came as though from under water, slow, ever so slow—"Go kill yourself."

Startled, I jumped, my muscles convulsing, my mind seeking escape. I watched my fear leave through the screen of the porch and then collapse into a thousand pieces on the ground outside, each piece crawling ashamedly through the black blades of lawn. Stranger stiffened, her arms stretching out from her body as if she were trying to stop herself from falling, the metal swing squeaking wildly as we both shook with fear.

"What?" Her eyes now open searched my face for familiarity. "What was that about curses? Do you know how to cast them?" she asked, nervously looking about the porch as though expecting to be overheard by someone.

"I was talking about curses, not spells. There is a difference. You know that, don't you? Spells are suggestions. That is all they are. You give a suggestion to someone, and they do the rest. That is why they don't always work. A curse, on the other hand, is like the answer to a prayer, granted, not a very nice prayer, but nonetheless a prayer. God, the devil, angels, or any other spirits you can think of are asked to contribute whatever force they can to cause a living being to act because of the influence they exert. Most people, of course, pray for things or positive influence. But there are those who pray for bad things to happen to others. I wish you were dead! I wish I had a dime for every time those words are spoken each day. Think of it this way; there is a good and bad side to everyone, right? Now if there is a good and bad side to people, then why is it so difficult to understand that spirits have the same characteristics? After all, they were once mortal themselves, for the most part. So what you are doing with a curse is asking those who have influence on a particular person to unleash their negative power. That's what happened to me."

"You've been cursed?" she asked, leaning her head once more back onto my outstretched arm. "That's simply wonderful! Now who are the ones who are supposed to influence you to do whatever it is you are supposed to do?" She wrapped her arms around her shoulders as though giving herself a hug, pulled her legs up onto the swing, and lay against me. "Tell me more. I find religious experience fascinating. Don't you?"

I had not thought of being the recipient of a curse as a religious experience before she mentioned it. I also believed I'd asked her what seemed like years ago now if she believed in curses. I couldn't see any reason that curses couldn't be classified as a religious experience; they have many similar characteristics, the main one, of course, being faith.

Butcher's favorite topic was faith. Oftentimes after church and Sunday school, we'd meet up at the park. There on the swings, we'd discuss the goings on at our respective services. It was on just such an occasion that he informed me that the Lutherans were onto us. The Pope had better watch his step because he wasn't just going to waltz into the United States of America and take over. "We've fought the Nazis, the Japs, and those pinko Commie bastards, so don't think we can't fight some old guy in a fairy hat. Reverend Smith says we'll kick his ass if he tries anything."

I didn't think for a minute that Reverend Smith said "kick his ass" or that the Pope didn't have anything better to do than come to the good old U.S.A. and fight with a bunch of Lutherans. Butcher got like that when he was excited. He seemed to like to fight or argue; it seemed to make him focus. I usually changed the subject and pretty soon he'd calm down.

"Butcher, do you have faith?" I usually tried to ask him a question when he got like that because it made him stop and think rather than just react. Thinking always seemed to calm him down. We were in the park playground where we spent many of our evenings sitting on the fabricated seats listening to the screech of rusty chains. He began to swing, me sitting next to him waiting. I knew what he was up to. When he didn't have an immediate answer, he'd confuse the issue by doing something else, giving him time to think. "Well?" I asked as he pumped past me, his feet pointing to the sky, his head lying back so his hair nearly touched the ground.

"Faith is believing in what you can't see. It's kind of like believing in air. You can't see it, but you know it's there because if it wasn't, you'd fall down dead."

I knew what he was saying. I'd thought along those same lines until Sister Mary … What's-her-name gave us a different slant on it. "Faith," she said, "is a belief in something that defies all the laws of nature and man." She went on to explain what she meant. "There is no way to prove we have a soul or there is a heaven or hell or that God exists at all. To believe in these things, we must overcome scientific reason and believe a power exists that is greater than the powers that can be explained by man."

The explanation, when relayed to Butcher, met with his approval. "Sometimes you Catholics get it right," he said. "I guess when old Martin Luther picked up and split, he left you guys a little something."

I didn't buy it for a minute. If faith is believing in something that cannot be explained, then it lives on a different plane in a different environment and, therefore, can't be used like some monofilament fishing line to pull things from the vastness of the spiritual world into the hard and fast reality of the physical world.

Butcher often said, if you can't see it, it doesn't mean it doesn't exist. "Close your eyes." And then he'd laugh. The thing he wouldn't see is that those things were there when you opened your eyes; therefore, they always existed.

Stranger and I sat on the swing until the sun glowed orange over the neighbor's house. I don't remember sleeping, but I may have. My arm was asleep, her head having cut off the circulation. I tried pulling it from behind her head, but it felt like it no longer belonged to me. I woke her in the process.

"Was I asleep?" she murmured, "I don't remember being asleep." She rolled onto her side, resting her head on the metal arm of the swing. She made a strange face when her head touched the cold metal but soon closed her eyes, pulling her knees to her chest with her arms and remaining trussed in just such a position. I raised myself from the swing with a minimal amount of squeaking. She opened her eyes as I stood but said nothing. She closed them again and murmured "bye" as I moved toward the screen door.

It is peaceful in the morning. The quiet in a city is unusual, an occasional bus, truck, cars, but for the most part quiet. The grass on the boulevard looked greener than usual, the asphalt blacker, the sidewalks cleaner. The trees that lined the boulevard looked proud, their roots slipping beneath the concrete and tar to steal nutrients, their leaves shimmering in the first rays of the day. It's the first few hours after you cross the line that are the most enjoyable. You get tired, your eyes begin to play tricks on you, but then, as if by some miracle all the cobwebs are blown away; a tornado came through and swept them away. It is like the eye of the storm. That quiet where you can hear an ant walk across the floor, the spider slip along the web, the mouse slip through the hole beside the door to safety—it's the clarity. It's as if you can hear every note just as clearly as if you were the horn itself. Everything is possible and nothing is impossible. Life seems a glorious thing.

Butcher and I often walked home from school together. We'd go down the alleys; the backyards of the houses were so much more interesting than the fronts. It was like being privileged to a neighborhood of secrets. Backyards are like family rooms, confessionals, where front yards are like parades and gala balls. Pomp and circumstance I believe they say. We'd creep down the alleyways, invisible, listening to the real lives of those who lived in the houses. The shouting and screaming, breaking dishes, and howling dogs all blended together, voices mingling like those at the gates of heaven waiting to get in. Sometimes we'd do things just to see if anyone would notice—trade a garbage can for another one, take a pink flamingo from one yard and put it in another. No one ever seemed to notice or to care.

I miss most of all walking with Butcher; most of the time when we walked the alleys, we did not speak. It was a rule that we followed, but we never spoke of. The alleys were our own world, where we were free from grown-up rules, a place where we could be who we wanted to be, what we needed to be. We'd sit on the ground, our backs up against a wooden fence and listen, listen to the lives of those we could not see but only hear. It was like listening to broadcasts from other planets, other solar systems. We realized we were all right. Our families, as screwed up as they were, were no worse than others. We learned we were okay, or as okay as anyone else. We laughed, we cried, and we held each other, praying in our own way that the lightning would spare us. We studied dead squirrels, scat, and the wonder of ants. We shared the lives of others, and it brought us closer together.

We would peer into the lives of those who barricaded themselves from prying eyes; the loose board, the knothole, or gaps were all portals into the secrets of those who lived invisibly only feet from us. Studying the contents of garages through the dust-covered glass of doors was like reading someone's diary We found a succession of abandoned and worn-out objects too emotionally charged to discard, hanging from hooks, rusted nails, and old coat hangers. An old bicycle, sled, toboggan, rakes and baskets, and trophies lined up along the walls collecting dust, fading from memory.

The garage behind the house on Pinot Street was our favorite. It was a converted carriage house that architecturally matched the stately house it served. A large multi-roomed house, stucco and brick, steep slate roof, dormers with leaded windows, it was out of place amongst the more modern edifices that had sprouted like mushrooms in the fields of this once respected farm. The horses once sheltered within its walls had long since been replaced by obsolescence. The old man who lives in this house no longer traveled farther than the front porch, where he could be seen most days asleep in his rocker, newspaper covering his knees like a blanket.

The building now housed remnants of a life no longer remembered, or if remembered, no longer considered relevant. It was another time, another place, simply a piece of a puzzle that made up our history. On the back wall of the carriage house were two small windows near the ceiling. The putty that held the glass in place was dry and brittle, and when the wind blew, the glass would rattle a tune; between the two windows, now purple with age and curtained with cobwebs, hung a moose head. It was our favorite find. The soulful head appeared to be sticking through the wall as if the animal had pushed its way in, looking for something to eat. It had large hand-like horns with fingers pointing upward. Its nose was black, nostrils large and deep, but it was the eyes that we found the most fascinating.

It had large black eyes that no longer sparkled with life but looked out on us through a veil of cataract dullness. They followed us wherever we went as though someone, something inside was watching us. It had small ears for the size of its head. We both ran frightened one day when a mouse poked his shriveled face from its pointed shelter and looked at us. The place smelled of age, mold, old leather, horse lather, and soap—not the kind of soap you bought today but the kind that was made from lye and lard, boiled to froth, its scent working its way into the wood like termites.

It was here in the presence of time past that Butcher and I had our first fight. We'd fought before, mostly words, hurt feeling, and disagreements that could and would be mended over a turbulent night's sleep. It was different that day; I don't know why. Maybe something bigger than what we spoke of loomed in our heads like sugarplums. I could not see the purpose of displaying a head, animal or not, on a wall. It made no sense to me. Killing something, not for food but for the perverse pleasure of having killed a living thing, stuffed it and mounted it on the wall as a symbol of virility made no sense. Butcher saw it differently.

"It has nothing to do with virility or manhood or any of that crap you always spout. It has everything to do with the rituals of man. We are not that far descended from the time when killing and dying was one and the same. It is no different than wearing a ceremonial robe of fur, a headdress of feathers. It has to do with sacrifice, atonement, and life, and it has to do with the right of survival, the propagation of the species. It has to do with man being an animal, killing and being killed. The trophies are reminders of a time when life depended upon death. We no longer need to kill to survive, but perhaps we need to survive to kill." Butcher seemed unusually agitated for some reason. I don't believe it was the mouse. We hadn't seen it upon our return.

I did not see the necessity of killing to prove anything, least of all to immortalize the past, a time most wanted to forget, and most did. If evolution were to be of significance, then leaving the sacrifices behind was essential. I could not see how killing and sacrifice any longer had relevance. Cows were shot in the head, chickens raised in cages, and vegetables grown by machines and chemicals; it made no sense. "You are full of shit as usual." It was only possible to break through Butcher's defenses if you got him off guard. He was stubborn, and no amount of persuasion would bring him around. It took ingenuity and, most of all, profanity to get his attention. "Killing some animal to prove that you are human makes no sense. I don't care if it is ritualistic or psychotic, it makes no sense." I had crouched down, my face a short distance from his as I delivered my response.

He hit me in the nose with his fist and walked out the door.

We avoided each other after that. We stayed out of each other's alleys. I know the incident wasn't entirely his fault. The more I thought of it, the more I realized that there had to be more to it than stuffed heads on the wall. His anger, although directed at me, came from some other place. We are all guilty of taking our frustrations out on others.

Cecilia I believe had done it to me. I wish she'd slapped me or punched me as Butcher had done. It hurt for a little while, and then the bleeding stopped after a few short minutes, and it was over. The only sign that something had happened was a few drops of blood on my shirt.

I could wash it off or throw it away; it would be gone, finished. Cecilia's curse, however, could not be dealt with as easily. I could not wash it off or throw it away. Her incantation, like a Druid's prayer, would not leave my thoughts. Her words pushed me in a direction I could not avoid, a maze of possibilities all leading to the same end.

As I sat on the floor of the carriage house, nose pinched, looking up into the nostrils of the great beast whose effigy hung above me, I wondered if Cecilia realized what she'd said or if it was just an outburst where the words flowed of their own accord. We have all been guilty of saying things without thinking, saying things we wished we could take back. But we can't. The hurt has been done, the words searing their meaning onto the spirit of another like an iron; the letters a blackish brown like burnt toast still smoking, stinking of burning flesh, there for all eternity.

Do you think it possible that words by themselves have the ability to change someone's life? Do words, once uttered, have the ability to unleash a force greater than the words themselves, like a rhyme whose meaning is dependent upon the cadence? Is it possible to take back those words and therefore the meaning?

When Butcher struck me unexpectedly and the first drops of warm blood rested on my lip tasting like sweet and sour sauce, even before my hand rose instinctively to my nose, the words *go to hell* formed in my mind. I did not speak them, nor did I try to erase them. They disappeared of their own accord, driven by my pain to the far reaches of my mind. Need the words be spoken to be relevant? Those who pray think not. God hears their words even if unspoken. Then why cannot all words be afforded that respect? If words and meaning are not linked inextricably, then one can exist without the other.

Meaning is often nebulous at best. I have heard it said that the Eskimos have seven different meanings for the word *snow*. The words for *sky* and *heaven* are the same in Spanish. Perhaps words have only the meaning we give them. Perhaps life and death are the same; one cannot exist without the other. Heaven and hell are each irrelevant without the other. I did not wish Butcher to go to hell, and yet my thoughts may have sent him there despite my protests. My only hope is that God, Butcher's God, wasn't listening.

I hear Cecilia's words, as well as see her face, when I close my eyes. I can see the pulsing of the vein that runs up her neck and disappears behind her eyes. I watch as her pupil's dilate, and words form on her lips and are thrown at me like darts. I have relived the event many times and cannot believe her curse to be an accident. I cannot believe there is more than one meaning for, "Go kill yourself." It is not the kind of phrase that we customarily inherit from repetition, like "Go to hell" or "Screw you."

Butcher and I did not speak for some time after that day in the "house," as we came to refer to it. In the weeks and months that followed, things were not the same, nor would they be again. I returned to the house often, but he was not there. I had been frightened on one occasion when someone began to open the door to the carriage house and then, for some reason, changed his mind and hurried off. I thought it was the old man and, after that time, rode by the front of the house to see if he sat in the sun in his chair.

One day when I returned, the head was gone, as well as several of the old, fat, tired bicycles. A lawnmower whose handle had been lodged against the front doors was also missing. I heard shortly afterward that the old man had died. His visiting nurse found him on the porch, asleep forever. I no longer felt comfortable returning to the house after that. Butcher and I spoke of it once, as though it had no more relevance than Sunday's football scores.

I lied when I told you Butcher had died—how he'd died. He hadn't died in the truest sense of the word, but he was dead as far as I was concerned. He died that day in the house as the mouse crawled from the ear of the moose head. He died the day the blood ran from my nose. He died the day I told him to go to hell, even though I never spoke the words. He died as the door was slammed shut and the sound of a squeaking hinge pierced my heart like an arrow. We took different paths after that day, paths that would run parallel but were destined to never cross.

Butcher's brother, died that day at the house, and even though there was no way Butcher could have known of his brother's death, I know he did. He was in the Army and had been in the war only three days when he was killed by what Butcher told me was friendly fire. He was dead nonetheless. I was not surprised; his fate was known to me. We sat on the swings that day for the last time, our heads back, our feet pointed to the sky, swinging in unison. I felt weightless, as though I could jump and never come down. Butcher's eyes were closed as though ashamed, tears finding their way across his face.

Butcher and I saw each other from time to time but rarely spoke. And then I never saw him again. I heard he moved to a different town, different school, and different friends. I heard his father and mother couldn't live in their home anymore. It was too difficult. I was told they wanted to leave it all behind, start over, like being born again. They wanted only to forget, if forgetting is ever possible.

Just before Butcher's brother left for boot camp and Butcher and I parted under the dull gaze of the moose head, they'd had a party, a farewell party. Butcher told me to stop by, so I did. We ate cake and drank pop, and everyone looked happy and nervous and agitated all at the same time. Butcher's mother broke into tears for what seemed no reason at all. When I was leaving I said good-bye to his brother, but Dick didn't answer. He looked at me, and I looked at him, and then I turned and left. Thinking back on it now, I think he knew. I believe I knew too, and I know that Butcher knew.

It's strange how many ways there are of dying. We tend to lump them all together so we don't have to broach the subject except on the most basic of levels. I believe we tend to fear physical death the most, although that is only one of the ways we die and, to me, the easiest. We are programmed after all by our pasts to live to be a hundred or die when we are twelve. Of course, there is the odd accident, a war, and always the chance we will become the target of revenge or madness.

How we can become so afraid of the inevitable is difficult to understand. It's like being afraid of summer or winter, or the occasional spring. And besides being inevitable, death is also the point where we cross over—where we get to meet this God we are so fond of talking about. Maybe that's the reason we are so afraid of death. It's not that we will be leaving; it's that hwill be waiting for us.

I am not afraid of death; I see no reason to be. I don't fear God because I don't believe He exists. Or if He does, I can't bring myself to believe He'd judge me for being human. After all, according to all the good books, He created us, and He either has to admit He made a mistake or cut us some slack. No, leaving our bodies is the easy part. By the time most people die, they are more than glad to be rid of them. Things stop working, parts forget what they are supposed to do, and people begin to reconcile their lives in terms of the number of steps to the bathroom.

Killing yourself is illegal; I find that extraordinary. I read in the paper about one man who failed to die after taking a bottle of pills; he was revived at the hospital and was arrested and placed under supervision for being mentally unstable. The assumption is that to want to kill yourself is insane. I believe it is just the opposite. When you consider suicide, you are forced to consider not only what is best for you, but for society as a whole. When someone risks certain death to save someone, we consider him a hero. When one risks certain death to save himself, we consider that insane.

Johnny J is my neighbor. He lives across the alley. I broke his front porch window once with a BB gun. I didn't mean to. I shot the BB into the air, and when it came down, it broke—I should say cracked—his window. At least that is what his father told mine. Johnny attempted suicide with a bow and arrow. I couldn't believe it when I first heard it. He was in the hospital for a couple of weeks; apparently the arrow had pierced one of his lungs. I went to visit him but wasn't allowed to go in. The nurse said he was resting. I looked through the door when the nurse went in, and he was just watching TV; maybe he was too embarrassed to talk to me.

A policeman was there asking question of the nurses and a doctor. Even though the incident was being treated as an accident, someone was not convinced. I had to admit I was not convinced. How does one shoot oneself in the chest with an arrow? I did a reenactment for my own benefit, and I don't see how it could have been anything but intentional, maybe stupid, but intentional. Looking down the wrong end of a target arrow is no small thing. It is not as difficult as I would have imagined. I was surprised that you could actually pull the string back, nock the arrow, and shoot so easily. Johny's shooting became, like so many things, not a question of how but why.

Unless you were trying desperately to be the first recorded case of death by self-inflicted arrow, it seems a rather risky and difficult way to die—that is, if you were serious. He was found on the basement floor with the arrow hanging limply from his chest. He'd apparently tried to pull it out before he passed out. Johnny J was like that. He could never make up his mind about anything. He was always afraid of being wrong, and I don't know why he worried so about it; he was always wrong.

Clifford, Johnny's cousin, whom I knew slightly because he lived next to Johnny and would shoot with us once in a while, told me about Johnny J just a couple of weeks before he went missing. I hadn't seen either of them in some time. I hardly recognized Clifford standing in the aisle of Super Save looking intently at a box of cereal.

He and Johnny J enlisted in the Army together, one of the buddy programs that allowed friends to enlist together. They'd been in basic training together in California and were to go to the Middle East together. The purpose of going in with a friend was that you'd look out for one another. Clifford said it didn't work out that way. Clifford didn't pass some test having to do with gas masks, smoke, and a lot of shooting. And anyway, he said they kicked him out. His exact words were, as I recall, "psychologically unfit." He didn't seem at all upset about telling me about it, so I guess he couldn't have been too upset. He left Johnny J there, alone in the desert.

Clifford said he got a letter from him afterward telling him the story of what really happened. I remember the headlines in the paper—"Local Soldier, Missing, and Assumed Dead." According to Clifford, Johnny wasn't dead at all, just lost. I remember the story well. The patrol Johnny J was a member of was ambushed; everyone was killed. Clifford said he assumed Johnny J was also killed because although they never found his body, he was a part of the unit and no one survived. Clifford said he'd gotten lost. He'd been driving a truck in a convoy. The sand was blowing, and visibility was poor. He was at the end of the convoy, his truck stalled, and he was left behind. Apparently no one noticed. When he couldn't get his truck started, he began to walk in the direction the rest of his unit had gone but got disoriented and finally crawled under a burned-out tank and waited. It took four days to find him; he'd gone the wrong way. It turned out that mistake saved his life.

I said good-bye to Clifford in the frozen food section of the Super Save store. His entire cart was full of frozen peas, eight ounce packages, Little Giant, I believe. Clifford had a smile on his face the whole time he told me about the exploits of Johnny J. By the time he got to the part about him getting lost, he was grinning like he was the happiest guy in the Super Save.

I made my excuses and left, turning quickly into the soups and condiments aisle; I left my partially filled cart at the end of the aisle and just walked out the door. The evening air smelled good, even in the parking lot, where discarded Wonderbar wrappers chased each other, playing tag.

I never knew why Johnny J tried to kill himself, if he actually did. Although I could never come up with an explanation for an arrow in the chest other than suicide, there may have been one. Johnny J and I were never that close, especially after the BB gun incident, and I didn't really care if he'd tried to do himself in or not.

I was curious about him and wondered whether he'd ever known Cecilia, but the more I thought of it, the less likely it seemed. Johnny J had less to do with girls than I did; they were afraid of him I believe. He was always saying, "What?" in an annoyingly loud voice when anyone asked a question. Not many people knew why he did that. I think they thought he was just strange or couldn't hear. It was kind of both actually. His parents were both deaf. Their speech was distorted because of their hearing impairment, and I believe he just developed the habit of saying, "What?" in an attempt to understand them by having them repeat themselves. It was terribly annoying though.

I had asked Clifford if he knew what had happened to Johnny J after he'd been rescued from the desert. He said he'd been shipped back to the States after spending a few days in a hospital. He'd heard from his old girlfriend that he had enrolled in St. Norbert's, which is a seminary school for those wishing to become priests. Clifford was sure he was still at the seminary, or at least he hadn't heard otherwise. I hadn't even known he was Catholic. If I had, I may have prayed for him.

"God knows Catholics need all the prayers they can get." Butcher used to love to tell me that.

I haven't seen her face lately—Cecilia's, that is. It seems that, as time passes, her appearances grow fewer. I am not sure that is true; it may be only because I wish it were true. One does not need to be reminded that one has not yet fulfilled his obligation, his portion of the contract. In my last encounter with her—which I believe was Saturday, maybe Sunday, a few days ago at any rate—she asked me how I planned to do it.

"What?" I asked, somewhat taken aback by her boldness. She usually said nothing at all and then this. "What?" I believe I repeated myself, sounding something like Johnny J. But I wasn't quite sure I understood her. Had I decided upon which way I would do it yet? It seemed entirely too personal coming from the one who had put me on this path. Was it not bad enough that she had condemned me like Lucifer to wander on the fringes of reality for as long as I dared walk on this earth?

She has stopped coming to me in my dreams. Now, when looking back on it, I rather enjoyed the dreams. I was sleeping with nothing much else to do anyway. They seemed to bother me very little, really!

As of late, she has taken to coming to me in the form of advertisements. I don't generally like endorsements, although some of them are quite entertaining. She has taken to placing her face on the bodies of others, I suppose in an attempt to get my attention once more. She reminded me just the other day by inserting herself into an ad I happened to be looking at on the bus. It had been six years since she'd condemned me to my fate. Then suddenly her face was looking at me from a twelve-year-old bottle of scotch with her face on the label, a typical advertisement in my opinion, lacking ingenuity, insight; but most of all lacking interest.

Dealing with her as I walk about in the real world is more difficult than when she was in the real world. It's not as difficult now as it was the first time she appeared to me ; I guess one can get used to anything. She always asks the same question, so that no longer catches me off guard anyway, she wants to know how I'm going to do it? That is the gist of it. She phrases her questions from time to time differently, I guess so as to keep my attention. It's like underlining a sentence or capitalizing it or placing it in an ad in *The New York Times.* "Have you decided upon a way to kill yourself yet? I'd sure like to know."

She seems to be getting more boisterous too. She used to whisper to me; I had difficulty sometimes trying to decide if I'd actually heard something or just imagined I had. Not anymore. Now she seems to enjoy screaming, waking me from my thoughts, making me wish I was already dead.

I fight her though. I refuse to be tormented by her. It is one thing to be responsible for something and another to think she have every right to manipulate the sequence of events to suit her ideals. It's no different than being hired for a job. What difference could it possibly make how the job is completed, as long as it is completed satisfactorily? You are not being paid for each step of the process but the end result of that process.

I may have frightened a few people on the bus today when I told her to leave me alone. Those around me pretended not to notice, but the woman sitting next to me moved to the rear of the bus—not a forgettable moment.

Deciding how to do it—kill yourself that is—is not easy. You'd think it would be, because what difference could it make? Well it does make a difference and a big one. It's not that I care about myself. People who contemplate taking their lives don't care about themselves. But they care about others. Most people have the erroneous idea that killing yourself is a selfish act. Let me set you straight on that. Killing yourself—cursed or not—is the least selfish act I can think of. With the exception of a few careless souls who throw themselves off buildings and land on some poor, unsuspecting soul below or the occasional shotgun blast to the face, which requires total and absolute remodeling of the scene of the crime as they say, killing oneself is exacting work. We do not remove ourselves from the phone book just to make others' lives more miserable than they already are.

Taking one's own life takes planning, if it is going to be accomplished with grace and with the least amount of psychological damage possible. Avoiding psychological damage, you must realize, is not a simple task. When Johnny J got lost in the desert and survived the ambush, it was not the fact that he survived that caused him to be sent home for evaluation but the fact that he realized that his inability to do things correctly was the only reason he still breathed. His psychological damage was self-inflicted because he couldn't live up to others' expectations; hence, the suicide note. Not only do you have to be concerned with your untimely demise, you also have to be concerned with the psychological impact that demise is going to have on others. Johnny J drove off a bridge in December into the waters of the Mississippi.

Hangings are preferable to shooting. Shooting is preferable to jumping off buildings, unless anything larger than a small caliber gun is used; then it doesn't really matter. Pills, I have to believe, are the most considerate. There really is little difference between going to sleep and waking up and going to sleep and not waking up, except for the fact you don't remember not waking up.

Did you know that the majority of the people who travel alone do so with pills? I can understand. I can even sympathize. They really wish to depart with as little notice as a small ripple on a mirrored lake.

I haven't as yet decided, although Cecilia insists I choose. I cannot. It seems only fitting that a transition from the physical to the metaphysical be given one's utmost attention. After all, we only get one shot at it, unless we screw it up.

I have been working on my suicide note in the meantime. I feel a note is quite as necessary as the deed itself in not casting unwanted or unnecessary guilt on those who happen to be in near proximity to the event. They didn't, as you must realize, ask to be there. The note, as I have come to see it, is essential. One must, in many ways, become a writer or at least be able to copy the style of someone accepted as a writer. The note, after all, has to convey not only the reason you crossed over with no oars in the boat but also the reason you chose to leave the oars on shore.

That having been said, I don't believe it necessary that we let everyone off the hook. Some people at this time, our last chance, need to be set straight. If we cannot take this opportunity to set them straight, then who can? If your intent were to jolt someone into the realization that he or she is actually not a human being, with feelings and all the rest, this would be a good time. But be clear and be precise. Too many times, the cops, in an effort to get home in time for supper, sweep things like this into the alley for the unappreciated sanitation engineer to deal with in the morning. I suggest you write multiple notes, not necessarily the same if you are doing it for effect. There is nothing more alarming than confusion, and confusion is the child of doubt, so the more of the worthy you can impregnate with doubt, the more swollen bellies there are going to be. Incompetent cop or no incompetent cop, swollen bellies are difficult to conceal.

We must consider so many people ; it is unfathomable at times how anyone finds the time to swim to the other side. People are so willing to blame themselves for everything; sometimes they invent things to blame themselves for. That is why the letter is so important. It is one thing to bring the righteous down from their self-indulgent clouds and make them look reality in the face; it is another to let others revel in the blame that only we should be arrogant enough to embody.

I have started my note; I have the first few words—not too personal, not too vague. "Too whom it may concern." What do you think? Would you be offended by the commonness of the salutation? Or would you, as I am, be enamored by its aloofness? It is not easy to distance oneself from the intimacies that breed familiarity and, therefore, guilt.

I do not understand why people do not blame themselves for the random accident or the cancerous growth but are only too willing to rewrite the entirety of someone else's life if it is ended without an agreeable explanation. Somehow someone has failed in some way—something was done to the person or not done at all, something laughed at or cried over. There is no way to know, and yet we fight each other to claim responsibility for the result. Perhaps we emulate God in this respect, taking credit for all things while taking none of the responsibility.

It doesn't help the gravity of the situation when one has been tattooed from birth with the enormity of the penalty for outwitting natural causes. I say natural causes, in which I include even the most bizarre of accidents. Hell fires, we are assured by those of religious prominence, awaits those who cheat death by leaving of one's own accord. The flames wait to claim those capable of walking across the room toward the open window or remembering how the bullet goes into the chamber. Perhaps the religious are simply jealous of those who wish to return to dust on their own terms, not afraid of the consequences of impatience. If God Can't wait to see us, and we Him, then what can be the harm in arriving early. It is not like tea after all, where elaborate preparations must be made. You wouldn't turn someone from the door on a stormy night because he or she had not made a reservation, would you? Then why would we expect God to be any less gracious?

Today, I met a girl who I had not seen in … Well, it doesn't matter. She sat down on the seat next to me on the bus. She read a magazine, something with flowers and picket fences, and then she turned toward me, catching me looking at her. She looked so familiar. I couldn't place her at first. It wasn't until she turned and smiled that I knew who she was.

"Why you're ..."

"Yes, and you are ..."

Her name was Jeanine. She lived across the street from me in the strangest of houses. The house did not belong, in that its architectural profile shamed the surrounding houses, and I couldn't help but believe it had an influence on the family. It was a modern-looking home, whereas the others in the neighborhood were monuments to Midwestern tradition—peaked roofs, small rooms, boxes with triangles on top. Her house had large windows across the front and a flat roof that was covered with tar and small pebbles. It was coated with beige stucco, while the other houses were clad in painted wood. It did not belong but refused to leave.

Jeanine had the whitest skin I had ever seen. Her white, hairless arms were seemingly made of porcelain. We shook hands, hers cool, cold actually, as if devoid of life. Her fingers were thin; her skin clung to the bone like plastic wrap. I could never once remember seeing her outside during daylight hours. If she were ill, she never mentioned it. Her nocturnal habits were of no concern to me, except for the fact that her vampire skin was out of the ordinary, which I always remembered to appreciate. The family would go for drives on warm summer nights; that was when she'd appear. We rarely spoke, but she never failed to wave her birdlike hand from the rear window as she passed.

We became friends somehow that summer, sitting on the small retaining wall that protected the side of the garage from cars. We'd sit in the dark and watch the sky. We rarely spoke unless it was important. Neither of us needed to be entertained; it was enough to share the summer nights. We were the most unlikely of friends, and yet I felt us to be. Bonds between people exist sometimes for no reason. It was as if we'd shared a past neither of us remembered but had not quite forgotten. We felt comfortable with one another, knowing the other would not judge.

She told me of her mother, who also lived without the light. The large windows of the house, floor to ceiling, were covered by garish material, black with purple and dabs of orange, psychotically tasteless. I had seen her mother only once. She had skin like rubber, white like the full moon. Her lips were red, smeared with color; a circus clown or whore? They would walk like moles from the house, single file toward the car, eyes glistening with tear-like anticipation, skin glowing white, like dry ice. They'd climb into the Hudson, heads down, rear ends in the air as though entering a rabbit hole. Her mother spoke, but never in public, and never to a man.

"She's funny that way," Jeanine blurted, as though having read my thoughts. "What could I say to that?"

"So what are you doing these days?" I felt compelled to ask, not really expecting an answer.

"I work at a bank downtown, on Washington. You probably know the one, First Federal—large pillars out front, green and white logo. I bet you'd recognize it if you saw it." Her words came at me like stones and me just inches from her.

My shoulder that rested against hers recoiled instinctively. I hoped she hadn't noticed.

"I work downstairs in the vault," she continued, "with the safe deposit boxes mostly. I like it down there. It's cool, like a cave, or the basement of the church. Do you remember the basement of the church?"

I felt my shoulders relax, touching her once more. I remembered only too well the basement of the church. Jeanine had saved me from embarrassment on more than one occasion, waking me from a fitful sleep as the nun approached looking for those who had relinquished their spirits to the devil. Jeanine had become my guardian angel, my protector.

I pictured her below ground, moving about in her bent shuffle as though she'd lost a contact, her skin glowing brighter than the overhead florescent bulbs, her nose sniffling in time to the bulbs erratic blinking.

"Do you like it?"

What else could I say? I hadn't seen her in some time. Talking about the weather always seemed inappropriate, like asking how much someone weighed. Who cared? I had the overwhelming urge to touch her skin to see if it really was made of rubber.

Her red lips seemed to be moving, talking to some invisible friend, seeking advice perhaps. "Yes, I enjoy helping others. The most amazing people come in to retrieve the earthly possessions of loved ones, father, mothers, and others. There is so much paperwork to go through, and we check not once but twice to see they've got proper authorization. The most fun though is when a box has been unattended for a long time, and the holder has failed to make rental payments. We try, of course, to contact the box owners or their heirs in case there has been a problem. But sometimes we can't find anyone. Then we are free to open an unclaimed box and seewhat is inside, in case some direction on whom to contact or what to do might be inside.

"Most often, we find nothing that helps us—old bonds, a few two-dollar bills, some gold coins, stuff like that. Rings!" Her eyes grew large, her voice rose in pitch; I could tell by her reaction she was fond of rings, especially other peoples'.

"Find any valuable ones?" I tried to keep from sounding uninterested.

"Oh," she said, her eyes opening wide once again, as though she'd witnessed something surprising. "That isn't my job. My job is to catalogue all the objects in the box and place the contents in a different part of the safe.

"What happens to the stuff then?" I really did want to know despite the yawn.

"Oh, I couldn't tell you. That's not my job. I just put them in an envelope and put them in a box in the safe. And then I'm through." She smiled as though happy to be finished with other peoples' less than valuable and unclaimed commodities. "And how about you?"

Her words echoed in my ear as she was thrown against me by the bus maneuvering a corner. I could feel her bones poking through her skin; she was a mere skeleton, dressed so as not to frighten others. I don't like it when people ask me questions about what I am doing. I feel it is none of their business really. I might not feel as protective of my comings and goings if I thought they had some merit, but I don't. Whether I work at the gas station or am a brain surgeon at the local hospital really has nothing to do with the weather, and that is why they are asking me about my doings, isn't it really? They need filler, something to talk about that is safe.

Many things are safe to talk about. You could ask how my dog was doing, and if I didn't have a dog, you could ask if I'd ever thought of getting one. We could talk about the government. The government is always good for a laugh or cry. Everyone either hates or loves the government, depending upon his or her income level. It's really not too difficult to figure out just by looking at someone whether they are more likely to hate or love their government.

We could talk about anything old. Old is always good. Everything old is good, except for people. Old people can be tricky, and I'd suggest you avoid that topic. No matter how much people hated their father or mother, you might just catch them on the day they returned from the funeral and were overwhelmed by the feelings they believed they were supposed to have. But furniture, clocks, houses—all those things are good. Everything was built better back then, except for the watch you own and the house you live in. Nothing, I suppose, is perfect.

I always make the mistake of first asking people what they do. Then I am overwhelmed by a sense of propriety to be honest with them. I try to avoid, at all costs, being honest with strangers. I take even more precautions with people I know. The truth has a way of changing reality, like sunglasses. The truth is more appealing because you can see less of it. It also makes it more dangerous because, at some point, you have to take them off. I lied. "I'm a student."

"Oh?" She seemed surprised. She must have seen my reaction to her raised eyelids. "Oh, I mean you never really seemed all that interested in education or religion, for that matter. What happened to you anyway? I remember when we were young you seemed so confident, destined for something big. What happened?"

Being asked what happened before you've had a chance to say what you were doing is a real ego deflator. She was inferring, of course, that I had not lived up to my potential. I assume she hadn't seen my picture in the paper or heard rumors about my rise up the corporate ladder. I was not in celebrity magazine. Nor had I appeared on late night television promoting a diet or a workout regimen. I had not hit a record number of homeruns, thrown a winning touchdown pass, or won a medal in the Olympics. I, like millions of others, spent my time coping. I know that sounds sad, but it is true. I go through most days unaware that my world has changed. The differences are subtle and of no consequence.

"What are you studying?" she asked, I believe in a way to repair some of the damage. I could see in her eyes she'd noticed my reluctance to answer and wished to soften her approach, be more personal, less bankish. It wasn't her fault. I knew that. It is the way she is. She said what she thought, not thinking first of how it might be interpreted. She did not sugarcoat or embellish. She was frank; honest; and, I have to admit, the kind of person you'd like to slap at times. I was surprised by her critiques; I didn't take them personally. I believe she meant no harm. She just reported on the events of her life as a sports announcer reports on a game, neither adding nor subtracting relevant information about her life. So I have to admit I was surprised by the look in her eyes, the quizzical look that scrutinized me for my reaction. She must have learned a thing or two about people skills while observing clients in the basement of the bank.

I hadn't been studying anything in particular but was reluctant to tell her that. Doing so would likely only bolster the impression that I had been wasting my life. I had no idea what I wanted to do or where I wanted to go. Staying in school seemed the easiest choice. I had been in school most of my life; to continue was no more difficult than breathing. "Everything," I managed to say, "everything."

She looked at me with her head cocked sideways like a curious dog I once knew and clucked her tongue against the roof of her mouth. "What do you mean by everything?"

I thought it was a vague enough answer to fulfill all the requirements of her question, but she was not to be put off that easily, so I continued. "I mean, I haven't decided yet. I like all kinds of things; I want to know about everything."

Her mouth began to open, a question on her lips, and then she stood and pulled the chord above my head. "My stop," she said smiling. She put her hand on my shoulder, pulled sunglasses from her large purse, turned, and made her way to the rear door, feeling her way along the aisle, holding the backs of the seats she passed. She turned as the bus pulled to the curb; she waved her glove-covered hand in my direction and disappeared into the crowd on the walk. I watched her from the window; she pulled a folded hat from her purse and placed it on her head and, like a bodiless ghost, bounced out of sight like an escaped basketball.

She had asked the wrong question of course. If she'd asked what I was passionate about, I could have told her. Everything does interest me; I did not lie in an attempt to be evasive or secretive. It's just that because I find something interesting doesn't mean I find it inspirational. Being passionate about something means being altered by it in some way, being pulled to it as though by gravitational force. You think about it, talk about it, dream about it. It is a reason to get up in the morning; it is the thing that keeps you wading through the endless amounts of bullshit we are forced to deal with daily. It is a reason for living, and we all need that.

Her floppy, rainbow-colored hat disappeared around a corner, her face all but erased by the scarf across her chin, the sunglasses, and of course the hair, which hung over her eyes like that of a sheep dog. She was all but invisible to others and, therefore, to herself. She was free to be the Unknown Soldier who each day descended into the tomb below the bank and lived out her days examining other people's lives so neatly packaged in tin.

The bus pulled from the curb to the accompaniment of car horns. I looked above the door, and there, emboldened on cardboard, was the logo for First Federal—green and white, the white so brilliant I squinted as if looking at the sun in August.

What would it be like to know and accept one's fate? As she disappeared around the corner of the brick building, I felt an unexplainable loss, a hole in my life. And yet I had not seen her or even thought of her in years. Still she had recognized me, and I her. I looked down from the green of the sign, and there, sticking through the black rubber gasket of the door, was a piece of olive green canvas tapered on the end, a belt perhaps. I looked through the glass but could not see her face. Cecilia, I thought, the floppy striped hat covering all but her nose, the scarf covering her chin. "Cecilia?" My voice was a question directed at no one.

An old lady sitting just in front of me, turned and, looking over her shoulder, inquired, "What dear?" The old woman's face was white, white as new driven snow, her lips red, oxblood red. She wore sunglasses and a floppy hat of many colors; a lime green chiffon scarf stuck to the corner of her mouth. "Did you want something dear?"

I got off the bus at the next stop, although it wasn't my stop. I could walk the several blocks. It would do me good. I don't spend enough time outside. I don't get enough exercise; I know that. It is just that I don't enjoy being out of doors. The noise gives me headaches, and the air smells of rotting eggs and burning garbage. Bodies everywhere jostle for position, bumping into one another like dandelion fluff. I feel like I am going to explode. And yet today I needed to walk. I needed to get off the bus, out of that space, and into the light. As the bus drove off, it seemed to grow darker inside until there was only complete darkness, black. I turned and headed up the street, nearly knocking down the old woman with the floppy colored hat. Her red lips smiled at me through the white mask.

The diesel fumes made me feel nauseous. My eyes began to water, and a sense of fear gripped my throat like an invisible hand. The anxiety seemed as unnatural as a crocus appearing in the snow, loving it. I am not afraid of death, for I understand it. It is this fear that has suddenly appeared and threatens my complacency that has upset me. When you are no longer afraid of death, what else is there to be afraid of? Pain perhaps, loneliness, but nothing a bullet or a pill—one of which has become destined to be my way out—cannot cure. Whether tomorrow or next week or in ten years, it does not matter, for the results will be the same.

And yet a sense of fear descended upon me like a black cloud. It is not the rain that bothers me but the loss of clarity; the gray light has turned everything into shadows of shadows, a hundred levels of dust. It is the kind of thing that makes me pray, and yet I cannot, because I have no one to pray to but myself, and I am preoccupied at the moment, not listening.

Like a windup toy, I make my way down the street, those around me careful not to step on me. There is someone just ahead who seems to be leading the way, blocking for me. I follow him; he's small, not over five feet. I cannot see his face, only the back of his head. A flower seems to rest behind his ear, a daisy with white petals and a brown center the color of burned wooden matchsticks. I want to snatch it from behind his ear and place it in one of my buttonholes. It seems like the most logical thing to do under the circumstances. And yet as I reach and my hand gets closer, he speeds up, walking faster as though being able to see what I am about to do. He then begins to run, and I follow. Out of breath I stop; he stops. He turns, laughing, his short, prickly hair standing on end like charred pines after a forest fire. It is Butcher—the Butcher of then not now, the Butcher I knew before when I was more alive than I am now.

He does not say anything; it is as if he chooses not to speak. He waves and smiles and grows smaller there on the sidewalk in front of me, and then he is gone. Only a small, yellow flower remains where he once stood, a dandelion I believe. It begins to speak, or at least the sound of Butcher's voice seems to be coming from the flower. "How are you doing, man?" he says. "Long time no see."

Could it be that Butcher came back as a flower? Could all that nonsense about reincarnation—that we do get another chance—be true?

I look at the flower to be sure. People rushed past, unaware the flower was Butcher. I had to push one man to keep him from stepping on my friend.

"Watch it," was all he said.

"How you been?" The words came again, this time softer, as though he wanted only me to hear.

"Pretty good," was all I could say. "Pretty good."

A little girl passed, tugging at my pocket as though trying to get my attention. She held the hand of a young woman; I could not see her face. She wore a pancake hat with the fishnet veil pulled down halfway across her face. Pulled to an abrupt stop by the little girl, the woman turned toward me. I could see myself reflected in her dark glasses, my face, blank, looking back at me through a web that resembled a prison fence.

As I looked away, the little girl pulled the flower from the crack in the sidewalk. "Look, Mommy," she said holding Butcher up to her, "A sunflower."

The woman pulled the little girl along behind her like a cork, her head bobbing up and down as she hurried to keep up. "Throw that thing away," the veiled woman said. "You don't know where it has been."

The little girl obediently let the flower fall from her hand onto the street. She watched over her shoulder as a fat man in plaid pants stepped on it. The little girl, unperturbed, hurried to get ahead of the veiled woman, pulling her down the sidewalk strewn with litter.

"Hurry, Cecilia." The words rang like distant bells in the madness. "You know how Daddy gets when we are late."

The smell of popcorn—sometimes that is all it takes to bring us back, like a lifesaver thrown into the dirty sea. The smell of popped corn wafted across the walk into the gutter and down the sewer where it would not be appreciated or cause harm. The marquee promoted three men with large eyes, mustaches, top hats, and horns, one with a curly headed face looking deranged, laughter spilling from his eyes, invited me in.

"Can I go in and buy some popcorn?"

The girl behind the glass with the small mouse-like hole looked up from her hands. She'd been studying them as if they were maps, or as if she were reading her own future. She looked surprised, as though no one had ever asked her a question.

"You'd like to go in to buy popcorn, and then what? I don't know; can you be trusted?" She squinted to get a better look at me. "You look honest enough, but then, how would I know? I need this job. What if you were to not come out and they found out and I got fired or, worse, had to pay for your ticket? You wouldn't do that to me, would you? You don't look like the kind of guy who would do that to someone, especially someone who trusted you." She seemed overwhelmed by my request.

I didn't know what to say. I thought she was going to cry. I tried to comfort her. "No, I wouldn't do a thing like that to you. It was just the smell of the popcorn, and I was having a bad day; I thought it would help. I don't have time to see the movie, and I don't really want to buy a ticket just to buy popcorn. Is there a policy about buying popcorn if you don't have a ticket? I don't want to break any rules or get anyone in trouble. Do you think it would be okay? I feel like I really need popcorn, and soon."

She looked frightened at first, like I was going to yell at her or reach through the mouse hole and grab her and pull her through the hole and beat her. Her fears seemed to disappear when I asked her to help. Most people enjoy helping, even strangers, especially strangers; it makes them feel good about themselves. It makes them feel needed, important. "I could get it for you if you like?" she offered, her manicured hands folded before her on the black ticket counter. "I'll get it for you. I'm sure that will be all right. Just wait here and let me get you some. Don't go off. I'll be right back. Butter? Salt?"

She made me feel like a small child—a child she needed to bribe to keep from throwing a fit, a child who needed distraction. She slipped out the door behind her stool, and the door closed behind her. The door immediately opened. She stuck her head back into the booth and said, "Tell anyone who comes I'll be right back. Tell them, okay?" And she was gone.

I wanted to yell, *Wait*. But it was too late. What if she thought I was crazy, and instead of popcorn, she came back with a policeman or security guard and I'd have to explain why I was bothering this little lady about popcorn—why I was frightening her, intimidating her, when all she wanted to do was sell tickets and then go home and feed her stupid, shedding cat and go to bed until tomorrow when she'd sell more tickets.

I couldn't remember what she looked like. She seemed familiar, like Jeanine. I couldn't be sure. I'm no good with faces; too many of them. My reflection in the glass looked smeared, as though confused. I turned to leave, run, hide before the cops would come and beat a confession from me. I detested violence but also knew I would not give in. They would have to kill me to make me confess. I hated bullies, especially cop bullies.

"Here you go," she said, setting the stained bag on the counter. Butter was seeping from the bag, making the black counter seem even blacker. She pushed the bag toward the mouse hole and then stepped away as if afraid it might explode. "It won't fit through the hole," she said staring at the bag. "If I tip the bag, the corn will spill." Emphatically she spoke with reason as though she'd been in this situation a hundred times before. "I could take some out, but I have no place to put it."

"Eat some," I suggested. "Eat some."

"Eat some?" she repeated, as though surprised by her own boldness. Her hand quickly reached for the bag like a frog's tongue, picking a kernel from the top and then another and another until the bag was a third gone.

"Now, roll the top closed and push it through."

She again immediately did as I suggested, rolling the top shut. But as she pushed it toward the mouse hole, she stopped. "What about my money? You haven't paid for the popcorn. Extra butter! That will be seventy-five cents." She held on to the bag, squeezing the sides firmly, small pools of blacker than black forming on the counter.

"I'm sorry," I protested. "I forgot. Here," I said, rummaging through my pocket for change. "Just a minute. Here," I offered, pulling my wallet from my rear pocket. Looking through the folds, I found I had no money. I had used my last change on the bus and had forgotten I'd bought some things at the store the evening before. She watched as I folded the wallet and placed it back into the rear pocket of my jeans. "I'm terribly sorry. I forgot—No, I didn't realize I didn't have any money. I forgot I spent it all last night at the store and had planned to stop at the bank and withdraw some for the week, but I didn't. I'll stop by tomorrow and pay you. I'm sorry. Thank you for your trouble. I'll pay you tomorrow; I promise." I turned to leave.

She said nothing, just looked at me with a hurt look on her face. "Here," she spoke more loudly than necessary, "here take the popcorn. I don't even like popcorn. Take it." She tipped the bag on its side and pushed it through the mouse hole leaving a greasy trail on the counter top.

I reached for the bag, grateful; kindness is rare.

As I picked up the bag, she stepped back once more, her back pressed against the small door.

"See you tomorrow," I said, unfolding the top of the bag and letting my fingers sink into the kernels.

"Tomorrow," she said, beginning to spread the grease around the black counter with a handkerchief, the counter becoming more beautiful as she worked.

"Tomorrow," I said, placing the first kernel into my mouth. It tasted old.

An old man, unshaven and smelling of a night of cheap wine, held out his hand. "Can you help me, fella?" His voice was cracked and broken, like an old record.

"Here," I said, placing the bag in his outstretched hand.

"What in Christ's name am I supposed to do with this? You cheap son of a bitch."

I walked quickly away from him. I heard the bag hit the sidewalk behind me; some people can't be helped. Butcher said those very words once to me. They sounded sinister and selfish when he spoke them, and I told him so. He just laughed as he always did when he was nervous. He hated not having a comeback. He'd get me though; I knew he'd be up half the night thinking of some way to get back at me. He was like that.

The street seemed overly crowded. Cars, trucks, and buses all swarmed like mad bees toward some destination. I closed my eyes to keep out the pain from the shrill cry of brakes and horns echoing off the concrete walls; people on the sidewalk jostled like cattle being driven by an invisible rounder, pretending to not see one another, knowing their fates were all the same, seeking not to embarrass themselves through recognition.

I was swept up by the river of people and propelled along by their wishes. I fought to escape the torrent of madness and found myself in the doorway of Donna's, a small restaurant, void of customers and void of life. Donna sits on a stool, spinning first one way and then the other; she's reading the paper and juggling her coffee cup. The radio is so loud I can hear it above the cacophony that surrounds me.

She sees me, my hands cupped against the glass, peering into her empty world. She waves, beckoning me to come in, her hand flopping like a fish. I push on the door and step inside, leaving the sounds of the street to the street. She reaches absently and turns off the radio as she has done a thousand times. It is so quiet the refrigerator hums like a sleeping cat; the clock hands drag the defining click forward with each second; and the coffee drips, first one drop and then another, like a gentle rain.

"How the hell are you?" her voice like a trumpet piercing the heavens. "What can I do you for?" she continues, not giving me a chance to respond, not giving me a chance to catch my breath.

"Coffee," I say automatically, not knowing what else to say, "And toast."

She looks at me, her newspaper still spread before her on the counter, her cup poised in her hand. "You need to eat something, kid. You look like hell."

She pats the red plastic of the stool beside her like a tambourine. "Sit. I'll get your coffee right away. Just let me finish this story about the princess. She's something else, don't you think?" Her face is buried in the paper, her blond wig not moving, her eyes trained on the small print. "Well, ain't that something? It says here she's worth over twenty million dollars. How the hell can anyone be worth twenty million dollars? There ain't nobody worth twenty million dollars." She folds the paper leaving it on the counter, a picture of the princess looming from the smudged ink like a bad dream. She slides from the stool and slips behind the counter. She pulls a cup from a tray and pours the steaming black liquid into it. She sets it before me, the dull thud of the cup sounding like a paperweight as the marble absorbed its sound.

"Toast coming up!" she says cheerily, as though she enjoyed toast more than anything in the whole world. "You need cream and sugar?" She scrutinized my face, tilting her head first to one side and then the other, like a painter looking for the best light. "You're too thin; you need to eat more. You want I should make you up some of Donna's delicious scrambled eggs?"

Her question came at me like driven rain, I wanted to duck, to hide. But I couldn't. I couldn't be rude. I was taught there is no excuse for rudeness. She was lonely. She needed someone to talk to; I could see it in her eyes. She needed a son, a child she could take care of, pamper. But I couldn't be that child; I could no longer be a child at all.

"Well," she said, continuing to look into my face as she adjusted the white collar on her bright yellow uniform, turned on the radio and asked "What do you think?"

There is no place for rudeness. "That will be fine," I managed.

I watched her walk to the far end of the counter, her large hips swaying in time to a tune on the radio. She placed bread in the toaster, broke two eggs into a bowl, and began to beat them with a fork. "The radio says it's supposed to rain today. That's good for business. People don't have anything to do when it rains, so they come in here. It's nice. They drink coffee, and we talk." She continued to speak to me, but I couldn't understand her over the drone of the radio, which she had reflexively turned back on. I looked at her from time to time between sips of the bitter coffee; she never did bring the cream or sugar. My periodic glances reassured her of my attention, and she continued talking as if I could understand; that was fine with me.

The walls were covered with calendars, mostly outdated, some dating back to the early nineteen hundreds. She or someone had circled the similar dates and days of the weeks of differing years on the calendar pages in red. Several of the calendar photos had been altered. One sported bathing beauties whose faces had been replaced with the likeness of Donna. She wasn't wearing her puffed-up wigs in the photos.

I heard the bells ring as the door was pushed open, altar bells that called people to communion, a high-pitched tinkle like breaking glass that managed to get under your skin and make you want to scratch. From the corner of my eye, I could see the figure make his way to the counter and slide onto a stool. It squeaked appropriately as he swung his feet onto the rail.

"Be right with ya," she called from the griddle, her words crashing through the waves of the radio—turbulence throwing the notes like confetti into the air.

Coughing, guttural sounds of a demon exploded from the end of the counter and traveled like locusts toward me. I looked reflexively toward the noise; it was him. It was the overcoat, the stubble bearded man, the hand reaching toward me from the sidewalk. It was him. His eyes were black as a stallion's; his words—"Cheap son of a bitch"—slashed at me like whips. It was him; the crumpled stained bag lay beside him on the counter, empty. He cleared his throat, raspy like wood going through a chipper. It was him, making sucking sounds like that of a bathtub bidding farewell to the last of the scummy water. He raised his hand as if saluting one of the calendars. He tried to stand but could not; his feet tangled in the rail. He turned to look at me, his eyes like lighthouse beacons searching the darkness for help. I could hear the words coming at me like stones—"sonofabitch, sonofabitch, sonofabit…" He fell over backward, one arm reaching upward as though trying to grab God's lapel, the other clawing at his throat like a dog instinctively scratching.

She did not see him when she turned. Her eyes looked disappointed—another lost customer. She looked at me; I directed her attention to the floor with the tilt of my head. His eyes were open, staring at the ceiling as though he were counting the holes in the acoustic tile; his mouth was open too, and spittle, like a stream worked its way down his chin and onto the checkered floor. He lay perfectly still, like a painting, quite pretty really—a striking contrast of his distorted outline against the regimented twelve-inch black and white squares. His face was contoured. His eyes, no longer of any use, seemed to be slipping inside his skull, leaving deep crevice-like canyons across his face—bad luck scars.

Donna leaned over the counter, her ample breasts covering my newly arrived plate of eggs. She tilted her head to one side like a dog does when it doesn't understand. Small whimpering sounds came from her otherwise emotionless face. "You'd better call someone," she whispered.

Call someone? Who would I call? Who could I call? What would I say? A question hanging in the air like a quote frozen in time by circumstance.

She continued to stare, her mouth, too, open like a choir girl's, lost in a trance, unmoving like a porcelain doll. Her lashes began to pulse, at first slowly and then faster, as though trying to rid her eye of a foreign object. She jumped, sending a cup to the floor and shattering herself back to reality. She stood up. Bits of egg dotted her uniform.

She moved like a cat from behind the counter, moving past me like an apparition of Nurse Nightingale. She dropped to one knee and placed her hand on the wrinkled forehead, being careful not to disturb the eyes that seemed not to notice. She took a napkin from her pocket and dabbed at the edge of the open mouth, stopping the river's flow. She stood, adjusted her uniform, and straightened her collar, staring at the face below her. "Popcorn?" She looked at me as though I could somehow confirm its existence.

She glided past me once more to a telephone on the wall. She pulled a quarter from her pocket and let it slip like a pill down the throat of an ailing child. Her fingers worked across the numbers as though their memory had left them. "Hello. Hello. Is anyone there?" I heard the garbled response move past her ear and mingle with the sounds of the radio. "Who is this?" she inquired as though having dialed the wrong number.

I wanted to stay, but I couldn't. I had things to do—school; I couldn't afford to miss any more classes. I had to leave. I just had to. I reached into my pocket, remembering as I did so that I had no money. I made my way around my friend on the floor, circling wide so as not to disturb him. I pulled on the door ever so gently, watching Donna's reflection in the glass holding the phone, one hand on her hip, tapping her foot in agitation. The bells warned her of my departure, and she turned, surprised, beckoning me to stay, to sit down and finish my eggs, please! I could see the fear in her eyes, and yet I had to go. I had places to be, things to do. "Please," I could see the word being formed by her mouth, pleading, but I had to go.

"Sorry," I mimed, pulling the door open wider, afraid to look back.

"Come again." I heard her voice, a celestial voice becoming extinct as the door closed, the sound passing through me as though I no longer existed.

I hurried down the street, distancing myself from the checkered floor. I knew what would happen if I stayed. They'd come, first the paramedics and then the police. They'd ask questions, questions I had no way of answering. This shadow on the floor, this outline like a Picasso had the answers, but he would not tell. They would want a story, something to write down in their little books. Whether it was true or false would be of no concern, as long as there was a story, something to write down—something to justify a nameless man falling from a stool and dying on the checkered floor as if life were a game of checkers; he'd just been jumped by God.

"King me," I could hear Him say, and then laugh. It was Butcher's laugh, a good-natured snort, funnier than the thing being laughed at. His was a laugh that made you question the sincerity of its inception, its motives, as if it contained a hidden meaning that only a few were privy to. "King me!"

I had to look around to make sure Butcher wasn't there; it was so like him, hiding these past few years just to get even with me, following me, keeping an eye on me, looking for ammunition. That laugh that made me question why I laughed. That laugh reminded me so much of the overcoat on the floor, laughing all the way to the Promised Land. I couldn't help but smile.

I hurried past the shops, the snow barely forgotten and the windows full of summer clothes, swimsuits, hats with flowers; plastic people in shorts. If the police needed someone to tell them a story they'd have to find someone themselves. Donna could tell them a story. I bet she would be good at it having spent years mixing eggs and stories. They didn't need me to tell them what they wanted to hear. I didn't have time; I'd missed too much school already.

When I am at school I get the feeling that I don't belong there, no one recognizes me. I try to contribute, get involved, but no one seems to care much about what I have to say. Maybe if I were like the kid who sits infront of me, Michael—tall, handsome, and rich—maybe then they'd listen. Money does matter; it matters to those who have it and those who don't. It matters because it intimidates, confuses, and camouflages its true intent. With money and magic, it's all about timing—looking the wrong way at the right time.

But I am neither rich nor good-looking. All I have are my thoughts and feelings. I no longer have friends, or close friends. Butcher is dead; I know he is dead, even though I look for ways not believe it. I know when I see him every now and then that he is a figment of my imagination. I know he no longer has a body and he can't talk to me, but that shouldn't keep me from talking to him. Just because he is not here doesn't mean he couldn't be listening. Maybe I see him from time to time because he wants me to, needs me to. Why is talking to him different from talking to God? I see nothing wrong in it; he was my best friend, and I miss him.

Butcher didn't think of me as plain or stupid. He listened to me. We'd talk for hours, arguing, fighting; that's what we did. But when all was said and done, we'd forgive one another; we'd let our differences go.

Except for the last time; I don't know what happened. We never forgave one another. Maybe it was my fault, but I don't think so. I can't remember what we fought about that last time. I have put it away; I have forgiven him. Maybe I need to forgive myself. But forgiveness is hard when you can't imagine what you've done wrong. What would cause someone to strike you in the face and then run off and never speak to you in the same way again? I can't help but wonder if Cecilia had anything to do with this. She is pretty tricky; she has a magic of her own. A couple of times, I saw the way Butcher looked at her; she had something on him all right.

Five, maybe six blocks to go; I was sorry I got off the bus. I should have stayed. I've done that before, gotten off early, and I've always been sorry. Even though I felt like I was suffocating, I should have stayed. The feeling would have gone away, it had gone away before. I'm too impulsive; I know that. I act too quickly, I need to slow down, pay more attention, and then I wouldn't be five blocks away. It feels like five miles. I should have sat there, closed my eyes, forgotten about Jeanine, forgotten about the white mask with the red lips, forgotten about the canvas belt. But I couldn't. The pictures fill up my head like sand; they make me tired. All I want to do is lie down, fall asleep, go somewhere else. But I can't. Sometimes I am afraid to sleep; the dreams just out of reach are not mine.

Have you ever had someone else's dreams? How do I know they are someone else's dreams? Because I am not in them. Places and things of course, I don't recognize, but then, that is not unusual. What is unusual is that I have no connection to the dreams. It is as if I'm standing on the sidelines watching, a mere spectator. Things happen to other people in these dreams; they are hurt or chased, and all I do is stand there and watch; no fear, no happiness, nothing, not one emotion. I stand like a statue watching; there is nothing really to do but watch. There has to have been some kind of mistake, a mix-up. How else could I be having other peoples' dreams? It makes no sense.

I hate trying to get across Hennipen Avenue. You are expected to cross six, no eight, lanes of traffic, and the signals don't give you enough time. The sign says *walk*, and I walk. When I make it about halfway across, the walk sign goes off. No one quits walking of course, or you'd be stranded in the middle of the street, abandoned by the sign. You just keep walking, hoping no one is looking for a compact, combing his hair, looking at her smile in the rearview mirror; it makes me feel like a duck on the opening day of the season. I've tried running, and I still can't get to the other side before the sign changes. That *don't walk* sign—that orange, grotesque hand- appears and fills me with guilt, and it isn't my fault.

It's not that I'm afraid of being killed by a car; it's the pain I hope to avoid. Like I said, I know how I wish to die, and it is not at the hands of an inattentive driver. Being dragged down the street, my face pressed to the side of the muffler, my skin bubbling like grease in a skillet—this is not my idea of the way to go. So I am careful, not crazy. You have to be on the alert always in the city; too many are not.

It's not so bad once you get across; the library with its beautiful facade seems to massage the tension from you. The marble steps, the columns, and the statue standing guard give me a feeling of peace. I never pass this corner without going in. Most times, I don't read or do anything really. I just like to sit and watch people. And the quiet; the quiet is embarrassing at times. I hear all kinds of sounds I wish I didn't; you know what I mean, sounds that bring back memories you had spent years trying to dispel.

The library has the most comfortable chairs, soft cushions and large, padded arms. Large windows on one wall go from the floor to the ceiling, maybe twenty feet or more. I sit by the windows in winter when the temperature is twenty degrees below zero and the wind outside turns your skin to sandpaper. I sit in the sun and let it flow through me like birth itself—warmth that reaches into you and then through you like an invisible hand. It gropes about your insides until it finds just the right place and then it settles there. It makes you sleep—you have no choice—and dream your own dreams. It's wonderful.

I go to the library to see Pablo. He's the janitor, or I should say the custodian. He always looks so proper. His blue uniform is always pressed, his shirt spotless, his pants creased to perfection. I try to get there about twelve thirty; that is when Pablo eats lunch. He can't go until the senior custodian returns. Pablo sits in the vestibule, a small reading room just off the main lobby. He sits on a marble bench. When I come in, I sit next to him, facing the other way so as not to make him uncomfortable.

Pablo doesn't speak English; oh maybe a couple of words, simple ones, like "hi" and "see you." I don't speak Spanish, so we just sit and eat our lunches in silence. He seems pleasant. At first, he pretended to not notice me, but after a couple of days, he began to smile when I sat down.

Pablo looks out the window at the small tree in the courtyard a lot. He seems to be thinking all the time, figuring out problems. Sometimes I feel as if I could be sitting next to someone like … a patent clerk who was passionate about mathematics.

Pablo is a good listener like Butcher. I can talk to him, maybe because I know he can't understand me. Most days, he sits facing the windows, me facing the doorway. I talk, and he listens. I pretend sometimes he's a psychiatrist. I don't know why. I don't particularly feel comfortable around psychiatrists, or I don't think I would. I have never been to one, so I can't say for sure. It's something about the environment I think that bothers me. The couch, lying down, the psychiatrist busily writing on his pad while you disappear a piece at a time—it is all too messy. I like the room with the granite bench. No one ever comes in during lunch. It's very peaceful.

Pablo smiles once in a while, so I know he's listening. I told him about Cecilia and the curse. He seemed to understand. Many people from Mexico have a feeling about things like that, spiritual things. They even have the Day of the Dead. We have Halloween. Their families celebrate the lives of those who have gone before by creating shrines in their honor; they place mementos of their lost loved ones' lives in the shrine, along with food and beer to celebrate. Here, we put flowers, sometimes even real ones, on graves, but not on Halloween.

Pablo attempts to be very punctual. He most often sits down to eat at exactly 12:30 p.m. and goes back to work at exactly 1:00 p.m. circumstances allowing. He eats one half a sandwich and drinks two cans of soda. He leaves his broom just outside the door of the room. He begins sweeping the foyer immediately after lunch. He has a routine that never varies. He sweeps from right to left in a diminishing square pattern. He never picks up the dirt until he has completed his route. He then mops the area with a series of scallop moves that are precise and astonishingly similar. He is an artist. I watch until he is nearly done with his floor, and then I lie down on the marble bench and look up at the arched ceiling. I close my eyes and feel the coolness of the stone enter my body like a thief, and then I fall asleep. I sleep only a few minutes; Pablo wakes me by routinely slamming the door of his cart.

Today, I waited nearly fifteen minutes for him to arrive. I didn't begin thinking of lunch; it would have been unfaithful of me; we always shared this time together. I watched the soda machine in the hall, red and blue, humming its erratic tune, a Navajo chant; he always stopped there before coming into the room. I wondered if he could be ill. He had not missed a day or been so much as a minute late in the times I had visited him. It was so unlike him ; something terrible must have happened.

I waited and waited and, finally no longer able to bear the agony, I left our room. I searched the halls; nothing; Pablo was nowhere to be seen. A receptionist sat at a desk facing the main doors. She busied herself with the answers to questions. Where might I find this or that? Where should I go? What should I do?

By the time I reached the receptionist the line had dissipated. "Pablo?" I queried. "Is he here today? Has he called? Has something happened to him?"

She looked at me, drenching me with a sense of calm, her actions robotic, her mood unchanged. "Pablo?" she repeated, as though I were asking for a book.

"Pablo, the man who does the floors, is he here?"

"Pablo," she repeated once more. "I have no idea; you'd need to speak to maintenance. They are in the basement, but you are not allowed down there without a pass."

"Pablo, the dark-skinned man—do you know him? Have you seen him?"

"I have nothing to do with the maintenance staff. You'll have to speak to maintenance in the basement. That is all I can tell you. Please move along; there are others waiting. Please move along."

I walked to the stairway at the end of a corridor. A sign on the wall by the door—white letters on a deep red background—warned unauthorized personnel not to enter. I pulled the large handle, and the door swung toward me, revealing a lighted stairwell descending down. A polished rail like a snake wound its way along the outer wall. I walked briskly down the stairs to the door at the bottom; a keypad at eye level greeted me. Codes—I like codes, mathematical sequences of numbers, a password. Of course literally thousands of variations are possible, but passwords are not about variations. They are about memory, the human memory. Passwords are simple, direct, and easy to remember—combinations that abandon the premise under which they were devised to accommodate the expediency of our society. The camera above my head blinked its red eye; I abandoned my hope of getting in and sat on the steps across from the door, defeated.

I did not have to wait long before the door swung toward me. A woman appeared. She stopped immediately upon seeing me, shielding herself with the door and obviously afraid. Her words were hollow, as though coming from a cave. "What do you want? You aren't supposed to be here. You have to be authorized to be down here. What do you want?" Her words came faster and then stopped. She peered around the edge of the door to see if I was still there. I hadn't moved. "I'll call security!" she squeaked.

"I just wanted to find out if anything happened to Pablo, the guy who cleans the floors upstairs?"

She ducked back behind the heavy metal door once more. "I don't know anything about that; you'd have to talk to maintenance." She began to pull the door closed.

"Wait, wait. They told me this was maintenance. They said I could find out down here."

The door opened slightly and she revealed a portion of her face to me. Her hair was piled on top of her head, and she wore large, dark-framed glasses. The nails of the hand wrapped around the edge of the door were colored a soft purple, matching her lipstick. The one earring I could see dangling from beneath her hair was in the shape of a cross, gold. "Wait here. I'll see if I can find someone to help you." Her voice seemed less frightened, and the eye I could see, the one surrounded by blue eye shadow, had stopped its rapid blinking.

I sat on the steps waiting for the door to open. I waited five minutes, ten, and finally stood up to walk around the small vestibule; sitting on the stairs was causing my leg to fall asleep. I walked around in a circle for another five minutes and then knocked on the door. No answer. I knocked again, this time louder and hollered, "Anybody home?" But no one came.

I suspected the woman with the purple nails had slipped out another door, wishing to avoid me. I climbed the stairs and found myself once more on the main level. I found a chair along the wall and sat down. I'd wait to see if she'd come out. She never did.

I had to get back to school. As I was preparing to leave, a large man waddled down the corridor toward me. He had a mop over his shoulder and was pulling a bucket on wheels by the wringer handle.

I watched as he approached, his feet slapping on the floor. His face was down, and his lips were moving as though he were counting his footsteps. He had short hair that stood straight up, ridged, like artificial turf. He wore glasses that rested at the end of his nose; he appeared to be looking over the top of them. He stopped directly in front of me; the radio on his belt was angrily trying to speak in a garbled foreign language I could not understand. He placed his chubby hand over it, muffling the sound. "They told me to see you if I could find you. They told me you'd been looking for Pablo. Pablo is not here." His words were flat, as though he were reading from a card.

"Yes," I said. "I know Pablo is not here. That is why I asked downstairs if anyone knew where he was."

He did not look at me but continued to look at the floor. His radio continued to broadcast messages from somewhere. His ears had turned a bright shade of red. "You aren't supposed to go down there unless you are authorized. You need one of these," he said, pointing to his ID badge. His picture showed him looking down and to the side; I could see mostly the top of his scalp through the thinning, ridged hairs.

"Listen, I just wanted to know if something happened to Pablo. We eat lunch together, and he wasn't here today. I don't mean to cause any problems."

He refused to look at me.

"Do you work with Pablo?" I asked.

"Who?" he asked, as though he had no idea who I was referring to.

I dismissed his feeble attempt to confuse me. "He's a small man, about five feet tall, black hair, dark brown skin, and wears a uniform like yours. Do you know him?"

He began moving his head up and down indicating he did know him. "They told me to look for you. You'd be a guy with a brown coat and an orange scarf. Is that you?"

I looked up and down the hall and could see no one else wearing an orange scarf. "Yes," I replied, not knowing what else I should or could say.

"They said to tell you he isn't here today." He began walking toward the door to the basement. After he'd taken a few steps, he stopped once more. Without turning, he said, "His name isn't Pablo; it's Bill. We call him Wild Bill."

"But," I protested, "the name on the pocket of his uniform says his name is Pablo. You're telling me his name is Bill!"

He began shuffling once more across the floor, his oversized shoes keeping time to the movement of his head, up and down, slap, up and down, slap. He pushed the bucket against the wall and placed the mop on the floor, the handle resting against the wall. His head turned in my direction; his eyes remained on the floor in front of me. "All of our names are Pablo or John or Pete. We used to have a Joe, but I don't know what happened to him. It's the names that come on the shirts is all. Bill got stabbed, they said. He ain't coming back for a while. I have to do his job too now, they said. It's going to be hard." He pulled the door open and disappeared behind it.

I jumped from the chair and headed for the door, my shoes squeaking on the glassy surface. As I grabbed for the large, polished handle, the door was pushed open. His head tilted toward the floor; he did not look up. "Bill didn't get killed. They said he was lucky. They say his wife stabbed him. They say she didn't mean it. Do you know Bill?" He stepped back, letting the door fall shut behind him.

I wanted to ask a million questions, but what would be the use? Pablo would not be coming back. I'd need someone else to eat lunch with, maybe at school. I'd never really spent any time at the library there. It was in the basement of one of the buildings. It smelled like cat pee, but then, that was a couple of years ago. Maybe it was better now.

I heard the bells of the church ring as I stepped outside. I'd be late again. It didn't seem to matter much; no one ever said anything. I'd just sit in the back like I always do and try not to fall asleep. It was so hard to stay awake after lunch. It wasn't that I was tired. I can't explain it. I just couldn't keep my eyes open.

I was going to miss Pablo. It's hard to find someone you can trust. I could tell Pablo anything, and I knew he'd not betray me. It all seemed so strange, him being stabbed and all, and by his wife. It was hard to understand what might have happened. Hard to believe it was an accident. I was glad he wasn't killed; he could come back next semester. If I was still in school, I'd drop by.

Two blocks to go; who was I fooling? Certainly not me. I knew I was going to miss half the class and make a spectacle of myself going in. I decided not to go. What was I going to miss really? Art history? What good was art history ever going to do me? Art was something you liked or disliked. It is something you feel or don't feel. I'd not been impressed by some of the junk they'd told me is good, especially that modern stuff. I knew it was supposed to be representational, but of what? A glob of white on a red piece of paper doesn't, no matter how hard I try, become a refrigerator, the explosion of the modern industrial complex on a new world. I give more credit to the person's ability to write, to dream. Take a piece of junk in the street, give it a past, present, or future, and you've got art.

Don't get me wrong; art is what makes the world bearable. Art is everywhere, and it is as important as the air we breathe. It smoothes the edges, refines the noise, and defines the humanity that we accept just because we breathe. I think it sometimes takes someone else to show us what it is to be human, what it is to be alive.

We, from the day we are born, drift toward grayness—the grayness of a day in March when the temperature is just above freezing and the water falls from the sky in drops smaller than the head of a pin; droplets so small they make us want to cry. We seem to want them though-to want to stay inside, hide under the bed, and pretend the rest of the world has gone, that it has been wiped away by the mercy of a saner God than the God in our consciousness. We begin to accept gray; it is better than black or the sun, which is way too bright. We drift to gray because it is safe. It is not extravagant; nor is it morbid. We are afraid of both. We have been trained to fear color as being too flamboyant, too garish, too sexy. We are afraid of black because it reminds us too much of what lives at the back of our closet after the lights go out. So we settle for gray. We let ourselves be sucked into its blandness. We have even learned to appreciate the subtleties of darkness.

If not for art, we would all think and act like the color of elephants. We would grow as wrinkled as them and hope it all ends before we realize that gray is only the place between white and black, the absence of color. It is art, color, outrageous color that makes us stand up and take our clothes off and dance around in the rain. We can't help it. We lose control. Art makes us what we wished we could be, what we wished others wanted us to be—anything and everything but gray.

Butcher and I argued about art. He saw it as something on the wall, something on the page, sound, harmonious, waves beating against us, waking us from our premature sleep. I see it differently. I see art everywhere. We are all artists. We all create, we all destroy, and we all build worlds in which to live. Everything we do is art; that should be no surprise. Wherever and whenever something is changed, it is art. It is art because a choice was made; decisions made us go left or right, up or down. The outcome, no matter how simple or crude is a process by which we choose. If we choose to do nothing, that is also our choice; it is also art. Wherever there is change, wherever there is choice, there has to be art. It is what makes the world laugh and cry, live and die.

We have been taught to be afraid of color. We have been taught to be afraid of emotions. And yet, no matter how much we suppress our feelings, they refuse to stay buried. They float to the top, see the light, and are born. We talk of heaven, God's beauty, and all that other crap, and then go to meet Him buried in a black suit with a black tie and, if we are lucky, our own shoes. Do we really think that God will somehow find our attire outlandish and refuse to let us through the gates? Do we believe heaven has been zoned and only neutral colors are allowed? And yet, when we depict the devil and his homeland, we do so with the brilliance of red and orange, colors that makes us sit up and take notice. No wonder evil is so much more attractive than good. White is terribly boring; black is worse.

Butcher said I don't know anything about art. I have no formal training; I couldn't draw a circle without a compass and, therefore, should not be so pretentious when giving my critiques. Butcher couldn't understand how something like Warhol's *Soup* could be anything but trendy, populist infatuation that would blow away in time like the leaves of fall. Butcher could be such a snob at times. Yes, I can't draw a circle, but I can appreciate a circle. I know the difference between a good circle and a bad circle, even though I can't draw one. I know what I like and what I don't like. What else is there? I don't know why I like what I do. To me, that is not as important as the fact that I do. I don't need to know about composition, form, or creativity; these are all matters for the artist. I cannot control the outcome of their vision but only acknowledge its impact on my life. If music makes me cry or a painting makes me angry, I do not stop to scrutinize the brushstrokes, the tempo, the words' meaning. I take my handkerchief from my pocket and wipe my eyes or put my fingers in my ears. Art is like a virus; it creeps inside of us. We do not realize it is there until the fever begins to overtake our senses, and by then, it is too late.

The first of the raindrops began to fall, striking my face like tiny fists. I looked up to see them diving from the blackness in the sky, escaping their kidnapper, seeking freedom, returning to a world they are more familiar with. Those who walked beside me and behind me instinctively raised their hands to protect themselves from the assault. Some ran; some slipped under awnings; some ducked into doorways and pretended to window-shop. I was carried as if by white water under a canvas awning, swirling like debris in an eddy, eventually ending up against the pier like trash. I could not move. Cattle awaiting the inevitable, we were forced by one another to cooperate, for we had no choice. This was one of those rare occasions when we allowed others into our space. I could feel them tight against me, their elbows biting into my side. We shared an experience, talking to others who just moments ago we would have walked by like ghosts, now herded into a realm of fleeting friendship by water from the sky.

I see the chattle smiling. I am pinned to the window of the lingerie shop, my face pressed against the glass like a pervert. Their reflections are profiles of who they need to be if only for a moment.

"Nice weather."

"Hell of a storm."

"You work across the street, don't you?"

Their voices take on an air of familiarity, a recognition of humanity you thought only took place in mass graves and concentration camp ovens.

A little girl stands next to her mother, her blue coat pulled tightly across her chest, a white hat slightly askew. She holds her hand out, feeling the rain as it falls into her hand like wishes finally coming true. She pulls her hand back hurriedly as if playing tag. The wind blows, forcing us closer. I can feel the breath of the woman beside me. Her smell makes me weak, ill in an odd sort of way. It is not a bad smell; there is just too much of it. It overpowers me like too much sugar. I can't move. I no longer care if I ever move again.

The little girl turns, smiling, as though she has won the game. She looks past the faces smiling back at her. I can see her black eyes looking at me from the glass, her lips moving. "What are you waiting for?" I don't know what she means.

What am I waiting for? I don't know. I want to ask her, but then she is gone. They are all gone.

The rain has ceased. The sun now pushes the blackness to the north. Patches of blue sky and white clouds bloom above the rooftops like carnations. The woman behind the glass shoos me away like a fly, her fingers down like a broom. I am bad for business. I can't move, not yet. I need time. It's a free country, a public walk. I can stand where I will, can't I? I watch the people moving by once more, as if the sidewalks are moving; they avoid one another, no longer talking or seeing each other. They avoid the puddles as if they have radar, puddle radar.

I wonder where they are going in such a hurry. It fascinates me that everyone has somewhere to go—always going, always looking for someplace to go, never content to stay in one place. It is as if everyone is running away. Maybe that is what they are doing. Maybe they are not going anywhere at all but running away. But from what? Is there something capable of frightening so many people? Is there something so powerful it can cause people to flow like lava from their homes and business in search of safety? Here they are running past me, running away or to something. It is impossible to tell which by the frozen looks on their faces.

Why won't anyone tell me what to do? I stand here just watching because I don't know what to do or where to go, and no one, not one single person, has stopped and told me what is going on.

I hear the thud behind me, like dead thunder, and then again. I begin to count—one thousand one, one thousand two—and there it is again; the sound is muffled, close by but sounding so far away. I turn, and there she is looking at me, her fist poised to make it thunder again. She flips her hand at me once again, as though I was a piece of lint. I step from the window. A cold drop of rain falls from the canvas as I leave its protection, reminding me how things could have been much worse.

I am entering a tunnel, a man-made tunnel of plywood and two-by-fours, protecting me from the construction behind it. The roar of engines fill the space, the earth shakes like an earthquake as the machines walk across the ground. A new building, a better building, a taller building will rise from the dust; the present marches on.

What do you suppose was wrong with the old building? Did it no longer serve its purpose, its intent? Did it no longer look as we wished it to look? Progress, they say; down with the old and up with the new. Progress pushes past us as though it has a life of its own. Progress, they say on the news and in the papers, you can't stop progress, and yet thoughtful people do every day. Progress and prosperity—we see them like two star struck lovers walking down history's lane, like Dorothy and the Tin Man on the yellow brick road.

Change is inevitable. It is the one constant in our lives, and yet we refuse to believe it. We tie ourselves to tradition and culture to avoid having to peel back the bandages and look at the wound. We are confused; it is so easy to become confused. We are bombed daily with the notion that new is good, good is new, change is new, and new is change; we begin to spin like tops. Progress is associated with change and change with good; therefore, all progress is good. We delude ourselves because we can't help it. We can't help being hopeful, for without hope, we will wither and die. Everyone knows that.

I watch from beneath the plywood roof people walking in one direction, people walking in the other direction, as if confused, lost. No one I have witnessed has stopped to look, actually look. They assume this hole filled with steel and concrete will be progress. And yet, when the earth shakes and the building falls, then what? When people die among the screams and hellish sounds of tearing metal, where is the goodness then?

Are we left with progress that has gone bad like milk on a warm day? Dare we believe progress is possible? When evil turns like a snake and begins to devour its own tail, then and only then do we see change is not so simple. There is much more to it than blindly stumbling ahead, hoping we survive. Survival is rarely the result of luck. Luck carries with it its own rules, its own rewards, which it parts with reluctantly, because luck is no more than the belief that God is really behind it all.

If God is the one who controls the strings like a puppeteer, we really have no choice, nor luck. We are what we are because we believe in hope, but hope cannot exist simultaneously with a God who tugs at our strings in an effort to manipulate us. If we are in control of our destiny and subject to judgment, then we have to act on our own.

Cecilia's words are mine to accept or reject, only mine, not God's. He has nothing to do with it. If He intervenes, a contract between Cecilia and myself no longer exists. If that is the case, God is bluffing. He could not control the outcome and dangle the idea of free will like a free pass, like salvation, for there could be none. For what is salvation but hope?

We are betting on a life that can only exist in our minds because, in heaven, the reward for being saved, if anything, is personal. Each heaven is, in fact, what we wish it to be because it is predicated on the premise that heaven is happiness, and only we can know what happiness is.

"What's down there?" a voice, shallow and unsure as a convert's. His words bounce around the enclosure, hard to hear, hard to catch. "Can I see?" he asks, pointing at the hole in the wall.

I step back, and he places his eye close to the hole. He says nothing. He pulls back from the hole and then positions his eye once more near the hole as if looking through a telescope. "It's just a hole," he says in his jittery voice. The back of his neck pulsates like a beating heart beneath his skin, so black it is almost evil. "It's just a hole," he says again, as if he can't believe it. "There's nothing down there but a hole. I don't know what I expected, but it wasn't just a hole."

"They have to start somewhere," I say as he straightens and steps back, nearly colliding with a woman hurrying down the wooden walk.

He looks at me suspiciously, placing his head once more before the hole and closing one eye. "Damn big hole," he says, now seeming to study the hole more closely. "What do you suppose they do with all the stuff that comes out of the hole?" He looks at me questioningly, as though I would know all the answers.

"I don't know." I scramble for time. "I suppose they haul it off to fill in some other hole they don't want or need anymore."

He continues to look at me as though considering my answer. He furrows his brow slightly as though doing so would somehow help him to think. "That doesn't just sound right now does it?"

I had never thought of it really. What difference did it make?

"Damn big hole," he said, shaking his head. He walked down the wooden walk, his feet sounding like those of a horse on cobblestones. It was a damn big hole.

I followed him at a distance, watching him tap out his own rhythm on the boards beneath him. He ran his hand along the wall, seeming to draw strength from it. I could hear him singing something quietly to himself; I couldn't make out the song. As people approached him in the narrow tunnel, they moved to the side as far from him as possible. He didn't seem to notice; he walked as though alone. As he approached the end of the tunnel, his pace quickened. He reached a small portion of chain link fence, where he stopped. He rested his forehead on the wire; I stopped to watch. He looked into the pit for several minutes and then began to climb. The fence looked to be ten feet tall or so. He reached the top and slithered over as though he had done this a hundred times before. He lowered himself down the fence; his fingers gripped the wire like the tendrils of a vine.

I ran to the fence to watch him climbing down into the hole, slipping and sliding, the dust rising behind him like a cloud. And then he was gone; a section of the bank broke loose, an avalanche covering him. A ball of dust rolled into the air; a thundercloud, dark an ominous as an old tombstone.

A crane operator stopped the motion of the steel finger that pointed to the sky. The large metal basket that hung from the cable swung gently like a spider at the end of a thread. A loud shrill sound, a horn, clawed its way into my head, scratching until I closed my eyes to shut out the pain. The sound ended as abruptly as it had begun, the cloud now rising effortlessly and being dismantled by the wind. The operator hurriedly climbed down the metal ladder, his white hard hat glistening like a seashell. He and others picked their way along the rim of the pit like ants. They assembled on a platform that fronted a small trailer. The first man to arrive pulled open the door and began to pull from inside large plastic buckets that he placed along the side of the trailer. A second man pulled several shovels and picks from inside and laid their handles against the side of the faded metal of the exterior wall. The others quickly arrived, pulling small buckets from the black interior. They moved quickly to the buckets where they sat and began pulling sandwiches from the interiors, eating, drinking, and laughing.

Music drifted toward me from a radio one of the men had pulled from a pail at his side. They sat contentedly overlooking the pit. I attempted to scream, to let them know what had happened. I waved my arms; one of the men, seeing me, waved back. The music, the same song the voice was singing just minutes ago, surrounded me; my shouts went unheard. I began to climb the fence, my fingers locked in the web made by the wires. I saw one of the men stand. Watching me, he began to wave his hands back and forth above his head, warning me to stop. Suddenly the music stopped.

"Get the hell out of here, you stupid bastard." The words came from the cupped hands of the man wearing the hard hat. "You're trespassing. Get the hell out of here."

I lowered myself back onto the wooden walkway.` Yelling, I pointed to the bottom of the pit. "He's down there. He's down there, and you have to do something."

They just continued to look at me, all of them now.

"Get out of here, or I'll call the cops." This from a man who'd picked his hat from the ground beside him and rested it on the back of his head.

The music once more blocked my protests, making me invisible. *Freedom's just another word for nothing left to lose*-the voice was wild, contorted. I sat leaning against the fence, my back to the pit.

Those passing by shook their heads in disapproval and then quickly looked away. I was becoming more invisible each day. I would soon be no more than a face on an advertisement glued to the back of a bench—a nondescript, lifeless representation of someone, who lives because of ink and paper. They walked by, looking but not seeing, making up a past and present for me, just like that. Each passerby created me in his or her own image, like God; each wondered when it all went wrong, how it happened, and felt uplifted in some small incalculable way because he or she had escaped. Those walking past would not look into my eyes for fear of damaging the illusion, dispelling the notion that I was already dead but did not know it. Soon they would begin calling me Dick.

Perhaps they were right. Did they see something on my face that told them I was already dead? Had Cecilia not only condemned me to the role of victim and executioner? Had she also marked me in a way that I had not discovered? Was it possible that fear and happiness, like masks, displayed our spirit whether we wished them to or not? Why not death?

Maybe it is so evident that we choose not to see it. Maybe we could not handle the constant reminder that death is always the last stop, no matter what the destination. It could be that we are only able to see the mark of death on others when we have seen it on ourselves; we are then able to recognize it for what it is. Those walking past looked at me as though I was already dead; perhaps I was. I couldnot believe they did not see the man buried under the wall of dirt. Perhaps I did not see it either. Could it be the whole experience was nothing more than my imagination playing tricks on me? It has done it before. It would be nothing new. But this time, it was different. I can't quite explain the difference. Different shades of gray, but definitely a difference.

Our minds are capable of things we wish not to think about. Have you ever looked at one of those paintings where it looks like geese flying, and then when you change your focus, it looks like fish swimming, and they are both there on the canvas, but we can only see one at a time. I know our minds operate like that. If they didn't, we would most likely go crazy. We would be forced to live in that place between the geese and the fish where there is no certainty. We know both exist, but because we can't see them both, our minds allow us only to believe in the one we can see, the other but an illusion, a dream.

It could be I saw nothing. My mind may have played a trick on me. I can see down into the pit, the dust swirling like small tornadoes, dancing like jitterbugs across the bottom. It looks like a shoe. I can't be sure. It is quite far, I squint, and yes, it appears to be something that looks like a shoe and there, above it, a hand. Those sitting above looking down into the pit now stop eating and stare, one poking the other, directing the other workers' attention.

There, it moved. I know I saw it move. Now the workers are standing too, moving closer to the edge of the pit, and crouching slightly to get a better look. One of them—the one with the blue hat—picks up a stone and hurls it at the movement; it misses. The rest of them pick up stones and throw. One finds its mark. A squeal erupts, a sound chasing itself around the walls of the pit. It moves, not a hand as I had suspected, or a foot; it moves like a shapeless shadow and disappears into a pipe.

"I'll get the son of a bitch," says the man with the white shell hat, walking towards the large finger pointing toward the sky. "I'll get the son of a bitch."

The rest of them, no longer hungry, throw the remainder of their lunches into the pit.

I left, I couldn't stay. What would be the use? They didn't want to hear me; they would not believe what I had seen. The small man, the man with the purple skin, would be dead by now, suffocated. I couldn't stay; I could see him trying to breath, the dirt filling his lungs, his hands clawing at the earth only making things worse. Would he be missed? Would anyone know he was gone? Would it matter? Not to him! He would either be someplace, or he wouldn't. He would either meet his God or he wouldn't. I wanted to say a prayer for him, but I couldn't bring myself to do it. Nothing is worse, in my opinion, than hypocrisy.

I've heard it said that, with prayer, we risk nothing. If only I could believe that. You have heard the expression, "Be careful. You may get what you wish for." Wishes and prayers, after all, are the same. We do not, nor do we have the ability to foretell the results of a wish or prayer, the two are synonymous in my way of thinking.

Suppose that the prayer for rain is granted. The earth soaks up the water, and when a man attempts to run down its slope, it gives way, burying him alive. He is dead because someone prayed for rain. It is the consequences of the prayers or wishes that are dangerous. We don't consider consequences before asking. We are busy attempting to improve our condition or influence our destiny.

I'm also desperately afraid I might pray to the wrong God. I mean, it is possible, isn't it? I had a God, and Butcher, he had his God, and even though they were the same, they were not. I'm not sure it is possible to have anything but our own God. But suppose that you go up to a guy, you're in need of help, people chasing you, robbing your house, something, anything. "Hey, I need help," you say. The guy looks at you and says, "I'd like to help." You look at him more closely and say, "Well, I guess not. You're not a cop; you're a bus driver. The uniforms are pretty much the same." Do you think that guy is ever going to help you? You just called him a bus driver, as though that were the worst thing in the world you could be. He not only would not help you, he'd probably help the devil find you if you were hiding; that's what I think. So what makes you think it would be any different with God?

We like to think of God as human, don't we? If that was true, then why wouldn't God be pissed if you mistook Him for an imposter, not the real thing? I mean, there are a lot of Gods out there, right? Gods come in all kinds, shapes, and color; some even have differing philosophies. The whole idea of asking something from a God who's not really a God seems risky to me, dangerous, especially if the real God finds out. Know what I mean?

Praying can be risky, especially when you're praying for someone's soul. That is big-time stuff, especially if you believe it. Eternity is a long time, longer than we can comprehend. I don't think we should be fooling around with longer than we can comprehend. I think my mother taught me that; it's one thing for God to be pissed at you, quite another for Him to be pissed at someone because of you.

Now, I know what you are thinking. God would never do such a thing. He is just, He is kind, and He is forgiving. Maybe, but He is also God. Remember what happened to the people He told not to look while he annihilated an entire city, turned it to stone. And that was just for looking. Can you imagine what would happen if He caught you paying off the wrong guy, praying to the competition? Like Butcher always used to say, "There's hell to pay when you piss off the Pope." He wasn't often right, but I'd give him that one.

"I thought I told you to get the hell out of here." The voice was coming from above me. Looking down on me was a large man with a white hard hat. His face was the color of Mexican leather, oxblood. A long, black braid hung to the middle of his back. His arms were large, his hands like small hams accented with scratches, one finger noticeably shorter than the other. I began to tremble; I don't know why, I wasn't frightened. His hard face seemed to soften at what must have appeared to him to be a pathetic boy. His eyes no longer squinted down on me. Relaxing, I could see his eyes, the color of the spring sky. "Look, kid," he began, clearing his throat as though he were about to give a lecture, "you can't be here. You could get hurt. My boss asked me to tell you to move along. We don't want no trouble, and I'm sure you don't. So just move along, okay." He placed his large hands on his hips and continued to look down on me as though waiting for an answer.

"What about the guy down there, the guy who got buried under the dirt that broke off? What about him?"

His face hardened once again, his skin becoming taut, seeming to darken as he stared at me. "What guy?" he asked, his voice sounding far less menacing than it had moments before.

"I saw a guy climb over the fence, and when he was trying to get down the slope, it broke free of the wall and covered him. I tried to tell you. I waved and yelled, but you wouldn't listen. I bet he's dead by now."

The large boom swung toward us, the shadow racing across the ground toward the place where the man disappeared.

The man took off his hardhat and began waving it frantically, trying to stop the boom. He continued to wave, and when he realized it wasn't going to stop, he threw his hat at the pit. It disappeared into the dust below. "Jesus Christ," he said, running down the wooden tunnel. "God damn it to hell anyway." His words came to me as if from the bottom of a well.

I hurried away, at first slowly, and then quickened my pace; I needed to escape that place—the air like a sauna, thick and sticky, the smell of death coming to me through the dirt.

It was good to be out of the tunnel. The sun breaking through the ominous clouds reminded me of Easter Sunday for some reason. I wanted to cry. I passed by a hardware store window and then a beauty shop." Haircuts, Tinting, We Do it All," the sign proclaimed. I was tempted. I heard a whining sound, the sound of hurt, pity, anguish, and love all wrapped into one like a tortilla. There in the alley, two dogs were stuck together, the female no longer amused, the male confused. The back door flew open, and a large woman in a white apron spotted with blood came out. Seeing the dogs, she screamed as though witnessing her daughter being raped. She pulled the lid from a garbage can and threw it like a Frisbee at the coupled dogs. It missed. They seemed not to notice. She turned and hurried through the large steel door, a crack like that of a whip climbing the walls of the alley as the door hit the bricks. She returned, shouting and waving her arms, a pistol held above her head.

She pointed the pistol at the dogs. I couldn't tell which one. I could see her eyes close, her hand shake, and her finger tremble as it applied pressure to the trigger. The explosion frightened her more than it did the dogs, who remained joined. The recoil threw her arm into the air; in her excitement, she fired several more times. The bullets hit the building with a dull sound, like that of a fist hitting a pillow. Four, five, I counted the shots, six. Her eyes remained closed, and the dogs remained inseparable. The sound of breaking glass followed, a squeal, like someone being goosed, and then a shadow blocked the sun like that of a large bird. The thud was unmistakable; it was as if I had imagined a body hitting the ground. I could hear the air being forced from the lungs, the bones pulling free of the muscle, the muscle turning too much, like ground meat. The man lay oozing what looked like oil just feet from me, his eyes looking to me for help.

It looked as though he'd dropped from the sky, a parachute failing to open, a skydiver who would never dive again. I looked up into the sky, hoping for answers and saw nothing but clouds, clouds that looked like giant brains floating by in mock tribute. A bathrobe flopped in the breeze; it clung to the iron railing of the balcony above, white, no stripes, no stars. A slipper looked down on me, wedged under the rail, desperately hanging on.

The woman opened her eyes, gun above her head, hands trembling. She looked at me and then at him, as if caught in a dream, a dream where she had to choose. A smile crossed her lips, and she lowered the gun, pointing it at me. She pulled the trigger and pulled it again, the hammer rising and falling like a Montana oil rig. She looked disappointed. The dogs separated out of boredom. I began to run.

I ran without seeing, a blind man. Why I ran, I have no idea except that I didn't want to disappoint Cecilia. I ran from instinct, not fear. I ran from a sense of preservation long bred into my line. My body ran to free itself from me but couldn't run fast enough.

I didn't even realize I was running until I collided with the girl. We tumbled together onto the walk, me pinning her to the pavement. Our faces were but inches apart, her eyes looking into mine, more amused than surprised. I watched as she tried to breathe, but she could not. I rolled from on top of her, pulling her to her feet. A slight trickle of blood seeped from the corner of her mouth.

"I'm sorry," I said, my words flat, meaningless. "Someone was trying to kill me. I was trying to get away. I'm sorry."

Her breath was returning. She gasped short gulps of air as though starving and then bent at the hips, hands on her knees, her long, brown hair hanging like a towel about her head. I stood beside her, my hand on her shoulder. I could feel her lungs return to normal, her body relax. "Are you all right?" I didn't allow her to answer, "There's a bench over there, across the street. Let's sit down."

She followed me as though she had no choice as I led her, head down, across the empty street.

"Here, please sit down." I pushed her gently toward the narrow boards that formed the seat.

She was well dressed—a nice coat, skirt, and shoes. Except for the blood at the corner of her mouth, she looked as though she were on her way to some social event, a baptism, a funeral, a dance, a dedication; perhaps the new building. Her feet were pressed to the pavement. Her legs were appropriately apart. Her elbows folded onto her knees supported her down turned head. "Is there anything I can do? I'm so sorry."

She said nothing, preferring to look at the pavement below her. "My shoe—did you see my shoe?"

I looked at her feet; one of her shoes was missing. "Let me look. It's got to be across the street. Just stay here; I'll get it."

As I crossed the street, I could see the shoe lying in the gutter, black patent leather shimmering as if made of water, the silver buckle reflecting the afternoon sun.

The shoe did not look familiar. I looked up and down the gutter for the loafer to match the one she was wearing; nothing. My eyes prowled the walk; no shoe. I picked the shoe from the gutter; it was stiff as though new. It even smelled new. I'd seen shoes like this before, but not for some time. Girls in school used to wear them for First Communion. We'd walk down the aisle of the church along the bright red carpet, boys on the right, girls on the left, hands folded in front of us, our eyes lowered in adoration, marching towards salvation. I watched as pair after pair of shiny, black, buckled shoes walked toward the altar and salvation. I turned and looked at the bench across the street. It was empty.

I wanted to run. I could feel my muscles poised, my heart beating wildly; I waited for the signal like a horse in the starting gate. The anticipation, the freedom—it took all I had to will myself to be calm and think. I could no longer trust my body to do what was best, what was right. It reacted as though controlled by an unseen force. I needed to find a place to sit, a place where I could escape the onslaught of events that seemed to follow me as I moved toward the school.

I could no longer trust what I saw or did not see, what was real. I walked deliberately, stopping only for the red light that loomed like a red planet against the light blue sky. The sounds of the city were no longer audible, and a deep silence stripped my mind of thought, rendering it blank as a new solar system. The pounding of my heart now rang like cathedral bells in my head. I saw a doorway, dark, protected by a black door with iridescent orange and blue doodles. I pulled the tarnished handle and felt the calm of the dimly lit room wash over me. I could hear again.

The sound of glasses rattling in a sink filled my senses. A bartender washed the remnants of lipstick and dead cigarettes from their prismatic sides. I stood in the glow of twisted light, a hungover collection of distorted ad hawking beer, vodka, and whiskey; one blinked at me in code. My pupils grew larger as light pushed its way into them-intruders, stealing the light from the room. The stools along the bar were empty. A blur of shadows was at the far end—the bartender, little more than an apparition, a row of booths, dark as private dungeons waiting to be discovered. At a small table was a figure sitting alone; an island in a dark sea of peanut shells, cigarette ash, and spilled dreams. She waited; her hand gripping the worn edge, fingers caressing the cold plastic as though drawing strength from an artificial heart. I walked toward the table, no more able to resist than a junkie needing a fix. She looked up at me as I stopped before the table, her eyes sad and empty. "Sit," she said looking past me, blind, as though waiting for someone in the darkness.

"Hi," I said pulling the metal chair from beneath the table's top, its feet screaming like nails on a chalkboard. "Sorry," I offered, my hearing now sensitive, like raw skin raked by poison ivy. "I don't mean to intrude. I don't know why, but I feel I must sit here. I must be with someone."

She looked at me, her eyes still not seeing, but softer, understanding. "Please." She gestured with her hand, the long fingers naked—no jewelry, no color.

I felt compelled to sit, needed to, like one who finds a lost child, be responsible. "My name," I began.

Her hand, like that of a traffic cop's before my face, stopped me. "I know," she said. "Mine too." She closed her eyes.

Her fingers began to beat the tabletop, her fingers each in turn pounding the arpeggio rhythm as though plucking the strings of a guitar. She made me nervous. I don't know why. But I wanted to bolt, run once more, leaving the feeling that had its hand on my throat.

"I live here," she said. "I have to live here; I have no choice, just as you have no choice. I have no place to go, no place to be, and I've never learned to fly." Her eyes remained closed, and although her face seemed to remain frozen in trance, I could feel her smiling at me. "I am an alcoholic." Her statement startled me. I know it shouldn't have, I could feel her tension as the words left her lips. "I live here. I have to. I am an alcoholic." Her announcement hurt, as though she'd punched me in the stomach. "I gave up my life for a chance at something better. It was but not for long. My days were bright, sunny, and warm, and then everything began to change, imperceptibly at first, small unrecognizable changes that were not noticeable at first. The light had begun to fade, and the clouds rolled in, became fog. The wrong prescription gave everything an edge, fuzzy, not clear, ghosts of Christmas past." Her fingers began to beat faster, as though accompanying her flight into the future.

"I live here now in an effort to remember—to remember what I have lost, what I have forgotten, and what I need to make me whole. The smells, the sounds, the lights melt together like ice cream on a hot day.

They say I should avoid this place, places like it. Temptation, they say. I tried. I attempted to be what I am not. I attempted to be what I could not be; I could not hide from myself. I can only survive by knowing that the demons in the closet are only clothes, hanging, crumpled clothes, a game of light and shadow. I tried to run, run to that place between light and dark, between up and down, hard and soft, clear and blurry. I got lost. I could no longer tell which way to go. It all looked the same in the nondescript darkness between sleep and waking. I was frightened. I'd cry but no tears would come, no laughter." She sat up straight. Tilting her head back, she shook her hair loose from her shoulders, and it fell like water from a cliff. Her face seemed frozen between asking and forgiveness. In her eyes I saw sadness and on her face a hint of a smile but no tears, only regret.

"I wanted to end it all." She spoke to the ceiling, a collage of stamped designs, aging, peeling, no longer relevant. No one looks up anymore. "I tried. It didn't work. It didn't hurt until afterward, until I realized you can't hurt yourself when you are no longer capable of feeling. You can only hurt others. It is not the excitement, you understand, that you crave, but the numbness. You are not trying to hide but to become invisible.

"You look as though you understand. If you do, then you are special. You must know then that it is not that I wanted to be someone else; I just didn't want to be me. I know that sounds crazy. I thought I was crazy, but now looking back, I don't think so. Confused, maybe, not crazy; lost maybe, not found. I just wanted it all to go away, like the stars in the sky; it is so much easier when there is no beauty left.

"I was going to jump, jump into the icy water of the river. I had read that is an easy way to leave. The cold numbs your body; your mind, already numb, does not fight back. Life leaves like air from a leaking tire, so slowly you don't realize it is gone until it is, and then, of course, you no longer care. There is no beauty to cloud your judgment, no voices to call you back, only memories without pictures, a blank screen—a sky with no stars, a sun with no light, a rose with no aroma.

"But I couldn't do it. It wasn't that I was afraid of death or God or judgment or any of the stuff you are supposed to be afraid of. It was something much smaller and more insignificant than that. As I stood on the bridge watching the ice break from the banks and rush into the night, I heard a train whistle. I couldn't get it out of my head. It spilled over, and pretty soon, I felt my whole body shaking, the sound consuming me. And then the thoughts, like sprouting seeds, jumped, first one and then the other, being born, becoming real. Where was the train going? Who was on it? The questions came so fast the answers had no choice but to remain silent. I turned from the railing, listening, hearing patrons' voices, talking, laughing, and making plans for tomorrow. And I realized that I wasn't afraid of tomorrow, only today. Then a car came by, its lights bright, making me wince. As it passed, a small face, a child's face, pressed against the glass looking at me, confused and frightened. And then she stuck her tongue out, moving it around in a circle, and then she laughed.

"They were the smallest of things—the girl, the train, the tongue, the laugh—and they had nothing to do with me and everything to do with me. I could see clearly for the first time that being afraid of tomorrow only makes you afraid of today. Your only memories become those of the fears of yesterday and the day before, of last week, last month, last year. What is there to be afraid of when you are already dead? I live here. I am an alcoholic. I am no longer afraid, or at least that is what I tell myself. Only tomorrow will tell. What do you think?" she asked.

I didn't, couldn't respond; all I could do was smile in reassurance.

"Excuse me," she said, pushing her chair from the table and walking toward the back.

I watched her walk into the darkness, her hair bouncing to the rhythm of jungle drums, the color changing from blue to orange to green with each neon sign she passed. The bar remained empty. The bartender placed the last glass on the drying rack. The water in the sink was sucked down the pipes. He threw the towel over his shoulder and came around the bar. He was short. I could only make out his outline, fuzzy in the dim light. His hair stood straight like that of a frightened dog. He walked with a boyish swagger, one hand on the towel, the other hanging on his waist by a loop in his pants. I wanted to go but couldn't make myself. I was too young. He would make me leave. I meant no harm. I had no place to go. I wanted him to understand. I lowered my chin to my chest and placed my hand on my forehead as though deep in thought, covering my face.

"What'll it be?" The voice was high-pitched, young, and so familiar. I am no good at names; I can't remember names until I've been around someone three or four times. I just can't. Faces I can remember, or at least a sense of familiarity kicks in the second time I meet someone. But voices—I'm good at voices. I know who it is on the phone before the caller tells me. Most times, I can tell even when someone disguises his voice in an attempt to trick me. This voice I knew. "What'll it be? "What will it be?"

I took my hand from my face, lifted my chin, and looked into his face.

"She's something, isn't she?" he said amused, pulling the chair toward him and sitting across from me.

"We're buddies. Well, kind of buddies; she helps me out from time to time. I helped her that one time, and I guess she feels she owes me. You know what time I'm talking about, don't you?"

"The time on the bridge?" I offered, not really sure.

"She tell you about the time on the bridge when she turned her life around. Good story, don't you think? I almost cried the first time I heard it. She changes it a little each time she tells it, but who wouldn't? Keeps it from getting stale. We met on the trip. We both left about the same time. Different circumstances, but what difference does that really make, know what I mean? You given any thought to when you might be leaving? I sure could use another friend or two." The familiar laugh echoed through the empty room.

He sat slouched in the chair; he always sat that way, no matter how many times I asked him not to. It made him look stupid; he thought it made him look cool. He hadn't changed—his hair, those big eyes and funny ears. He hadn't changed a bit. "I met a friend of yours just the other day. She says to say hi. She wanted me to ask you something, but

I feel kind of funny about it. I guess it's because I made so much of it before, you know. It's nothing really; she just wanted to know if you'd forgotten. You know, you haven't, have you?" He ran his hand through his hair. "Well, I should be getting back to work."

The sound of a glass hitting the floor and shattering slithered toward me like a crystal snake. I looked to the rear, and from the darkness, I could see her coming. Her skirt swayed from side to side as she moved, as though dusting the darkness. I looked across the table, and he was gone, the chair empty. I looked around behind me and over at the bar. He wasn't anywhere.

"Can I get you something, hon?" The voice was distant, unfamiliar.

I looked at her standing before me, pad cradled in her hand, pencil poised. She looked familiar, so familiar—her yellow uniform, white collar. "Well, what's it going to be? I ain't got all day."

I picked up the damp towel from the table and walked toward the door. She didn't say a word. I heard her gum cracking, November ice.

I stood, steadying myself against the building, shielding my eyes from the light. Sirens screamed past. Fire trucks, a rescue squad, and police, eating sandwiches, drinking coffee, and hurrying to dig a dead man from the earth, only to have to put him back later. I stepped into the alley—into the shadows and the smell of urine, of something dead, not as bright as God's face. I wanted to be left alone. Was that even possible?

We are only alone when no one wants or needs anything from us, when duty and responsibility belong only to the boy scouts, when we are dust. We are haunted; we haunt ourselves with obligations real and contrived. Obligations make us feel needed and wanted; they give us reasons to delay becoming compost.

I see the school, its red brick facade orange in the afternoon light, its windows black, as though the glass had been painted. Like a photograph, it is still, all but the flag that waves in its own pursuit of liberty. The marigolds below a brilliant yellow, brighter than any sun, duck their heads in deference to the wind. The rope slapping the hollow pole sends shivers up its steel spine. Like the howl of a wolf, the song of coyote, it calls to me, "Come quick, before all the knowledge is gone. Come quick."

Gertrude waited, her eyes on me, her small octagonal sign flat against her thick thigh. "Hurry; hurry before the light turns." Too late, the green has miraculously turned to yellow and then red, as though I willed it to happen. Gertrude looks disappointed; she returns to the curb, the sign returning to her thigh as if it were a holster.

"Hi, kid," she said in her gruff voice—forty-seven years of cigarettes and brandy. She has a pin tacked to the pocket of her jacket, a gray coat with blue piping. "A dollar fifty," she says, "post office coat, Goodwill. What you think of that?" She likes me. I gave her my lunch from time to time; it was nothing much—an apple, a cheese sandwich, a box of old raisins. She's grateful, one of the few grateful people I know. "Been smoking since I was seven." She taps her gold pin with her wrinkled red hand. "Salvation Army, ten cents; I gave it to myself."

Gertrude no longer works for the school ; no need since the stop signal was installed. But she continued; no reason not to. The administration tried to make her stop. She threatened to picket the school, got a petition together. The district superintendant let it blow away like candy wrappers.

I could see the school, not the school that housed the art history class I was skipping but the one I attended with Ralph and Cecilia.

Gertrude lives above the drugstore across the street, pimple cream factory she calls it. She spends her days on her patio, sitting on her bench here by the new stop signal. When it rains, she stands under the awning; when it's cold, she watches the bench from her window.

"I thought you'd have quit this dump by now," she told me as the light turns green. "Wait now. Wait for me. Why you going anyway?

Christ, the day's about over. You'll be coming the other way shortly. Sit. We'll have a talk like we used to. You got a girlfriend?"

I'd known Gertrude for two years now. She seemed mean at first, but that is just her way. She reminds me of Eleanor Roosevelt. I have a picture of her in my history book. She has a long face like Eleanor's, jowls, glasses. I made the mistake of calling her Eleanor once; she slapped my ear. It hurt like hell.

"Why you so late? Dog eat your homework?" She liked to tease. She didn't mind when you didn't answer her; she expected it really.

She had two kids once, she told me. Either dead or missing; she said it amounted to the same thing. Her husband left too, she said. Went to the store and never came back. "Best day of my life," she'd said. "Best god damn day of my life."

"You should wear a hat," I said. "Ninety percent of your heat goes out your head," I said.

She looked at me and then hit me on the knee with her octagonal sign. "What do you think is going to happen? I'm going to get sick and die? Just think, you could have my bench. As a matter of fact, I spoke to my attorney this morning, and he said it's in the will. This bench you like better than school is yours. So don't be giving me any more of your shit, or I'll use the edge next time, and that will hurt like hell." You couldn't help but like Gertrude..

"So what you been up to?" she said, her eyes continually cruising the sidewalk for children approaching. She looked methodically at the sign every so often; it always seemed to be on yellow. When she was satisfied no impending danger was about to befall a child wishing to cross the street, she began again. "So tell me, damn it. I like to know what you young punks are up to; gives me something to think about. I've gotten to the place where my life ain't much fun anymore; I can't remember what I did when I was your age, so you've got to give me something to keep me going."

I never knew if she was serious or not. I found it difficult to believe she was lonely. She'd told me once she enjoyed her own company too much for that. She pulled a rumpled cigarette from its pack, pulled the filter from the end, and threw it into the street. She struck a match, touching it to the end that now dangled from the edge of her mouth; the paper erupted in a flame. She drew hard on the smashed cigarette, the end now a brilliant red honeycomb. She blew the smoke in my face, causing me to cough; she did that when I didn't answer her.

"Okay, what was it you wanted?" My eyes stung from the smoke, tears forming to wash away my sins. "What have I been up to? Well, let me see." Sometimes I made stuff up, like sports and school recitals. I wasn't too convincing, but she never said anything. I never really knew what to tell her. I wasn't embarrassed or anything like that; it was just that I hadn't done anything.

"Hold on now." She jumped up as a small girl approached the curb. She held out her hand to keep the child from stepping into the street, and as the light turned green, she held her octagon in front of her and began walking across the street, the girl in tow. "Come on, come on. We ain't got all day," I heard her chiding the girl.

Halfway across the street, the girl turned and looked over her shoulder. She winked and appeared to giggle and then continued to the other side of the street alone as Gertrude let go of her hand. She was wearing only one shoe; her other foot was clad only in a white stocking.

Gertrude fell onto the bench beside me, happy at having helped another child safely across the street. "So tell me. Come on, you must be doing something worth talking about. You ain't dead, are you?"

I wanted to tell her about Cecilia and Butcher. I wanted to tell her, but I knew what she'd say. I know what I'd say if someone came to me with a story like that, and yet it was true. "I saw a guy die today," I began cautiously.

Gertrude didn't look at all surprised. She went to take the cigarette from her mouth. The paper stuck to her lip, and her fingers slid down the creased paper and stopped on the honeycombed ash. "Jesus Christ." She began shaking her hand, trying to rid herself of the pain, the heat searing its way beneath the skin, one more scar to add to her collection. She placed her fingers in her mouth. "Go on, I'm listening."

"I saw a man climb over a fence, and a dirt cliff caved in on top of him, and I couldn't get anyone to believe me, and now he's dead."

"Did you do everything you could?" She looked into my eyes and then turned away to suck her fingers some more.

Had I done everything I could to save him? I don't know, maybe. Perhaps I could have done more, but they wouldn't listen. "I don't know. I don't know what I was supposed to do. When I saw the bank give way and cover him, all I could think about was what it would be like to be under all that dirt, clawing my way out, breathing dirt, and then nothing. I couldn't yell. I couldn't speak; I couldn't even pray." I wanted to cry.

"There, there," she said, taking her fingers from her mouth and patting me on the head. "I'm sure you did all you could. It wasn't your fault." She tried to comfort me, but I didn't deserve it.

I knew I hadn't done everything I could have. I knew if it were me down there, he would have done less. It is really all about us, survival, waking up morning after morning until one morning we don't. I don't know if I've got that many mornings in me. I'm glad now I didn't give him anything; my effort would just be down there under that dirt with him, not doing any good for him or anyone.

"I saw a guy die once," she said, placing her arm behind me on the bench. "A big bastard this guy was. He must have been maybe four hundred pounds ; I know you could hear the crash for blocks. It didn't really sound like a crash though, you know like you'd expect. It was more like a four hundred pound basketball being dropped off the roof onto the street—the loudest thud you can imagine. It killed not only the big guy but the woman driving the car. He ended up in her lap, went through the windshield. It happened just before I went on duty. I was watching from my window. I could see the whole thing happening. I could see it coming, and there was nothing I could do about it.

"Her kids brought flowers down here to the corner for a couple of weeks, asked if I'd keep an eye on them. I hated to leave them out there on the street when I went upstairs, so I took them with me. They looked really nice on my table, and besides, they weren't going to do her no good anyhow."

She patted my knee with her red octagon and then continued. "I know what you mean. I couldn't yell either. I wanted to warn them. I knew it was going to happen. That kid on the bike couldn't see. The girl on the handlebars blocked his view. He shot right out into the street. The lady was coming from over there." She pointed to the corner across from us. "She was coming through the intersection, and the kid shot right out in front of her. I could see it all coming. She swerved and ended up on the sidewalk. This big guy—he was standing there eating a sandwich with one hand and holding the folded newspaper in the other. If he'd left when the sign turned green, instead of standing there reading the paper, he'd be alive today if his weight didn't killed him; fatest guy I think I ever saw! I went right down, got there before the cops, before the ambulance. The car was sitting right there, just a few feet from where we are now," she said, once again motioning with her head toward the street.

"I didn't know what to do either. He was lying on the hood, half in the car, half out. The ground was littered with blood-spattered glass, and right here, by your foot, was the paper, folded just as nice as you please—just like he'd left it for someone. He was killed by the funnies, Dagwood and Blondie. Beats all, don't it? Killed by Dagwood and Blondie. When I tell people about it—and I don't anymore unless, well unless they're like you—they just tell me I'm full of shit. And I don't need to hear that; it's the truth. You believe me, don't you?" Her face looked haunted.

I could see no reason why she'd make up a story like that. "Sure," I said to comfort myself as much as her. "I believe you."

She smiled slightly out of the side of her mouth, like she'd had a stroke. "Funny thing," she said. "They never found that kid on the bike. I guess he didn't know what happened and just kept right on going. They found a shoe under the car but were never able to find who it belonged to. Little girl's shoe, or so they say. I never saw it myself, but they were asking about it; I know that. I had a hard time sitting on this bench for a while after that. I took to standing behind it, just in case. I'm over it now. That boy, the one riding the bike, he looked like that kid who follows you from time to time to school. Short kid, hair standing on end like he stuck his finger in an electric socket. Kind of a smartass. You know him?"

I heard the bell ring—long, drawn out, irritating as if on purpose. I saw the doors burst open; faces flew onto the sidewalk like a levee had broken. "I got to go," I said, rising from the bench.

"What's your hurry?" Gertrude mumbled, her fingers in her mouth, her other hand busily fishing a cigarette from the crumpled pack.

"I got a lot of homework," I lied.

"Not surprised," she said, "being that you never go to school."

"See ya."

"See ya," she said, putting the cigarette in the corner of her mouth and digging in her pocket with her raw, red fingers for the matches. I had not walked far when she called after me, "Tomorrow?"

I raised my hand to acknowledge her but stopped—the voice, the whine; I turned to see the waitress in the yellow uniform sitting on the bench reading the folded paper, laughing loudly to herself; no doubt Dagwood was up to something.

I didn't remember walking home. I'd walked home before, but not in a long while. I take the half-hour bus ride daily—a city bus, crowded, nothing to do but look out the window. The ride, although I often complain to those who will listen, is enjoyable. I do not like the closeness, smells, or the noise. Nor do I like the people, each rider catatonic, oblivious to one another, or the coughing.

Outside the window, the world passes, events observed and recorded as if a documentary designed to draw attention to the life that goes on around us that we do not see. Cars, trucks, buses, all jockey for position on the asphalt; the heavy scent of fuel envelopes us like an industrial perfume.

Most of all I enjoy the endless circus that flickers by, like scenes from an old movie, as I walk or ride. Faces, houses, dogs, cats, old men bent with age, fearful women, and smiling children all mill about the stage as though waiting—waiting for something to happen. I do not remember any of these things on that day. I do not remember walking through this play.

I awoke on my bed, legs stretched out before me, shoes shedding the city's grime on my new bedspread. The knock, the door opening with its familiar squeak, and my mother's voice pulled me from sleep. She'd been crying. Her tear-stained face looked at me and then turned away as if ashamed, pulling the door closed behind her.

My grandfather had died. I wasn't upset; to me, it was more of a relief. I know that sounds callous, but he'd been dead for some time if you must know the truth. I watched him die, a day at a time, an hour at a time, his memory being erased by age and disease. He would, in time, have no past at all. He would not be the person he had been. He would have ceased to exist; he would be dead. They would not build a monument to him. He would not be written about in history books. He would only be remembered by those who knew him, and in a few short years, they would disappear, taking him with them. He would become an etching on a stone, a name on a piece of microfilm; he would become a statistic, accidents at home.

He fell down the basement stairs striking his head on the concrete floor at the bottom. He died instantly they said. They refused to believe he was dead before the fall and insisted on reconstructing his demise; the law they said.

Grandfather had spent his last years wading through purgatory, living with my aunt and with us as he could no longer be trusted to care for himself. His world was not ours.

I watched as they carried him out to the ambulance, a nondescript shape under a thin blanket. Someone had given him a rosary; the bronzed Christ, nailed to the worn, wooden cross swung gently from the edge of the stretcher on its necklace of beads. Someone wanted God to help him remember.

My grandfather had been running away for the past several years. He had become a magician, disappearing from the house only to reappear later, on an unfamiliar corner. We would become part of the show, searching for him, finding someone who cared little about being found. He carried with him the present and only enough of the past to cause him to disappear. It was that past he searched for on his expeditions, not knowing it had been replaced by the present. He escaped often, creating a game that we all played, whether we wished to or not.

Now he was gone, no one to find any longer, one less person to deny our mortality. I see him in my dreams, standing on a corner looking into the sky, waiting for an answer that would never come. He is staring at a house, a tree, a rusting car, familiar landmarks like squares on a Monopoly board, helping him find the way home. I can see the fear in his eyes, the fear of a lost child, looking to others for help and receiving only pity, because pity is all we had to give.

My mother had asked if I wanted to see him, to say good-bye, him lying at the bottom of the stairs, his blood staining the floor. I could see no point; we had said our good-byes when we knew each other. Now saying goodbye would have no more significance than shaking the hand of a president. I declined.

They say when we die our spirits hang around a while so that they can say good-bye, or at least that is what Butcher used to say. He had a book on afterlife experiences he enjoyed reading to me. We discussed the possibility and probability of spirits. He believed they stayed; I could not imagine why they would want to.

"It is a process of letting go," he'd said, "a transition from one existence to another; it takes time." He was very emphatic on this issue, time. I could see his point. There was a change. But to what? After all, it was not like going shopping, looking for a new coat. We don't keep trying on new existences, like coats, after we die until we find one we like. He refused to see my point, and we'd part on a familiar note. "You Catholics have no soul," he'd say, and I'd respond predictably, "You're full of crap." Then we'd go home happy.

I do believe we stay around after we die for a time, but not in the same way Butcher believed we did. I could see my grandfather disappearing after his death a day at a time, until it was a year and then two, and finally, without realizing it, he had disappeared completely. Butcher was too pragmatic. Black is black; white is white. He could not distinguish between spirit, and spirit! To him, everything could be explained through definition, and if it could not, it did not exist. The concept that words can have many meanings was lost on Butcher because it was too irrelevant. It left too much room for interpretation. "What I am saying and what you are hearing may be two entirely different things. That is not the purpose of a word; words impose clarity on thought, not confusion." He could not see purpose in having many meanings for a single word. "Lutheran," I'd say. "Catholic," he'd reply.

We disappear gradually, but not because we are taking our sweet time about leaving. Rather, we disappear slowly because others take their sweet time about letting us go. We can take the leftovers of a life-the clothing, the old fishing rod, a hat, and put them in boxes in the attic or garage or give them to Goodwill or the Salvation Army. These along with the smells disappear quickly. The rest is harder, because no matter what we say and what others tell us, we don't want them to go. We don't want to put them in a box in the basement because they are a part of us. When they are gone for good, a piece of us goes with them; we become less than whole. We become one of the many meanings for love.

When people talk to me about spirits walking among us, I usually frown. My reaction is not conscious; I didn't even know I did it until one day I happened to see my reflection in the glass when Butcher was going on about a haunted house he'd read about. My face, as though it belonged to someone else, contracted, my brow forming ridges like a plowed field. My eyes squinting as though looking into the sun, I didn't recognize myself.

"Are you listening?" Butcher had said, obviously noticing my lack of attention.

I usually challenged him every few minutes during one of his stories, so it was no big trick on his part to tell I was dreaming of other things. It gave me a strange feeling to be looking back at myself, as though I were being spied upon by a stranger.

It isn't that I don't believe there are spirits here among us. I hope there are; it would explain a lot of things. People have no problem at all attributing their inability to explain phenomenon to faith. Then why not spirits? When someone sees a statue bleed or a crippled person get up and walk, it's a miracle. Suppose it's nothing more than a spirit playing a trick on us. If we can give all manner of physical attributes to spiritual things, like burning in hell, then why can't spiritual beings have a sense of humor? We assume that because we can't explain something it is either good or evil. Suppose it is just some spirit trying out a new comedy routine. They can't go around moaning all the time.

"Do you think it's possible that, when spirits are around, they assume the physical resemblance of the first person they come into contact with? What would be the point of even having a visible presence? It seems like it would have a negative impact on your ability to sneak around if people could see them—unless, of course, they do that to frighten us."

"Or," Butcher chimed in, "they are here to teach us a lesson, remind us of our own mortality. Just like the ghost and Scrooge."

"I was being facetious," I returned the serve.

"You aren't smart enough to be facetious," he said, pointing toward the corner of his bedroom. "There's one."

I turned quickly, and for just a fraction of a second, perhaps less, I know I saw something.

"See," was all he said, throwing his baseball glove at me.

The picture of Cecilia and I standing on the front steps of the school, dressed in our whitest finery, hair slicked back, shoes reflecting my world like a glass lake, hangs on the wall next to my bed. Sometimes I feel her watching me. It isn't one of those things where the eyes move and all that; it's more of a feeling, an invisible ghost. As I looked at the picture, it occurred to me that I never remembered seeing Cecilia smile, while she was alive that is.

She seems to have been making up for it of late however. And there's something about that smile of hers I can't quite put my finger on, but I know it's important. She actually seems much happier now than I ever remembered her being in school. Death is strange that way.

Cecilia's parents are dead; I don't know exactly how they died. There was a picture in the paper of a car crash, and my mother kept saying, "That family sure has had a streak of bad luck."

I always pretended I didn't hear her. I think they died in a car crash, but then maybe the picture was of someone else; so many people die in car crashes.

Their pictures were in the back of the paper, small black and white photos that looked like mug shots from their high school yearbook. I never understood why anyone puts pictures of people in the paper when they die, especially pictures that don't even look like them any longer. Her parents were fifty-six and fifty-nine respectively. He was nearly bald, and she had hair the size of a beach ball. In the paper, she had short hair, and he had more hair than Jimmy Hendrix.

I see Jimmy, Cecilia's brother, from time to time. He works at the supermarket. He's never been right. When he was about six or seven, somewhere in there, he was hanging by his legs on the gym set at school, and for some reason, he let go, landing on his head. They said he would be okay, but he isn't; you can tell. I heard he is living in a group home with other people who have become disabled. The medication keeps him fairly calm, calm enough to hold a job anyway. He was a mean little bastard when he was young.

He threw a rock at my father's new car and cracked the window. When my father got out he threw a rock at him. My mother used him as an example of what can happen to children, evil taking over their souls, the whole time I was in grade school. "See," she'd say, "that's what happens to boys who do evil things."

She refuses to look at him now when we go into the store. I think she feels like she had something to do with his misfortune. She probably did.

He sure is different now. His expression never changes. He doesn't seem to notice changes in the weather, or if he does, he doesn't react to them. He doesn't sweat when it's hot or shiver when it's cold. His body seems to have compensated for his injury. It must be similar to enhanced hearing or smell after going blind.

Jerome, my cousin, is blind. He told me that he could smell someone fart in church and tell you within a person or two who did it. I hoped so for his sake because he wasn't any good at all with his cane. He ran into more stuff than I did when I closed my eyes and wandered around the house. I think he did that so he didn't have to go out in public. He said he hated being around other kids who could see. They were always saying things like, "Did you watch TV last night?" or "Did you see that?" Those were the two sayings he hated the most. I could see his point.

It was almost dark. I couldhear my mother banging around down in the kitchen. She makes a lot of noise when she cooks. I think she is trying to make me feel guilty or something. My father will be home soon. My mother will call to me from downstairs, and we'll sit down like we do every night and eat. We eat in silence for the most part. Except for saying please pass this or that, we just eat. Most of the time, we don't say anything; we reach.

You'd think we'd talk; other families do. When I'd gone to Butcher's for supper, his family had talked. As a matter of fact, they talked all the time. It didn't matter if it was supper or not. I couldn't spend more than a few hours there and my head would begin to hurt. I began to think I was hearing voices, and that's not good. What was most troubling was they all talked at the same time; no one listened. When you have been taught like me to be seen and not heard, that is a problem.

Where Butcher's father was talkative, my father was not. Butcher's father seemed to enjoy all kinds of things. Sports, politics, you name it; he could talk about it. My father seemed to know less than anyone I'd ever met. Or maybe it seemed that way because he never said anything. He liked to listen to the radio. The radio was always on when he was home, and most times when he was not. He insisted upon it. He interacted with it like a guy with bad kidneys interacts with a dialysis machine. It put him to sleep at night, it woke him in the morning, and it entertained him all day long. He loved it; we hated it. It wasn't so much the radio as what was on it. He loved to listen to some talk show where the guys thought they were being paid to be funny; maybe they were. I hoped they weren't being paid much.

He also liked baseball. He never played baseball that I know of, but he seemed to love the game de facto. Most Saturdays and Sundays, our house was filled with screams from the announcer, who was accompanied by a pipe organ. To this day I hate *Take Me out to the Ball Game* and, of course, the national anthem, especially the anthem. It was bad enough when just the fans sang. Now they have some celebrity at every game who leads everyone in the baseball prayer. Just because you are an entertainer doesn't mean you can sing. And then each of them has to personalize the song in some way. Rather than rushing through it so as not to embarrass themselves, they drag it out, they change or forget the words, and they make it into something it was never intended to be, a commercial.

I could hear the TV downstairs; the sounds followed the stairwell, a wooden-ribbed chimney carrying the unwanted noise into my room, tracking me down. The TV was always on; a member of the family, it shared our meals, our lives. It filled a void or created one, depending how you viewed it. It kept our attention focused on the lives of others, which were easier to deal with than our own. It sucked the life from us, leaving us empty; I could feel it go. Sorrow, joy, envy, anger, all my emotions were seduced into leaving, becoming someone else's. I could feel the blue haze, its flickering spirit stalking me, slithering up the steps in search of its prey, slipping under my door and across the floor, and me breathing it in. I could feel it entering my lungs, burning like hate, stealing my thoughts until I no longer had the will to resist.

"Supper!"

I can watch the street from my bedroom window. It looks over the front yard, the walk, and the treeless boulevard; only the flat graying elm stumps remain. The street is a black river; a moat that separates us from those who live on the other side. From my other window, I look into the side yard at the plum trees, old and gnarled. I can see a rose garden, my mother's, the envy of the neighborhood, framed by a white picket fence, a burial ground for the squirrels who died at the hand of my father; they were attempting to steal the tulip bulbs nestled against the foundation.

The yard is a painting, vibrant colors on a background of green, Picasso's dream interrupted by a wooden fence intended to keep me out. And yet I could look down upon the neighboring yard as if a prison guard, seeing all, hearing everything, as though I had a direct line. The naked young wife of a cop, oiled and golden brown like a Christmas goose, waiting for the adulation she knew she deserved but never got. The words, angry, hateful, threatening, streaming through my open window on those summer afternoons, grabbing me, making me watch, making me listen. She was leaving; he was throwing her out, but not until after the party.

"Hi, how you doing?" they would say when we passed on the walk, he holding her arm.

"Fine, good, wonderful." I never knew what to say because I knew; I had looked into their world. By winter, they were gone. The summers would never be the same; I hope the party was a success.

"Supper!"

"Coming!"

I looked at the picture just to make sure. As of late it seemed to be changing, not much, just slightly, but enough. At first I thought it was simply fading. After all, it was an old picture; light was hard on old pictures. But then I began to realize it wasn't the entire picture that was disappearing, growing lighter, but just me. And Cecilia—she appeared to stand out a little more, and her face appeared to have the slightest hint of a smile. I hadn't remembered that. And Ralph—he began to look more and more like Butcher. His hair, now cut short, stood straight; heavy, rimmed glasses protruded from his shirt pocket; his left thumb was wedged in his pants pocket, cool.

Supper was uneventful. The TV talked and listened for us, and we were left the simple task of placing the food in our mouths. "The Virgin Islands," the announcer said, a buzzer sounded. "What are …?"

I watched my mother tense with embarrassment. She was embarrassed by pretty much everything or appeared to be. I think really she was embarrassed because she thought she was supposed to be. Words, pictures, thoughts—all were labeled, a propriety index, which she referred to without thinking, acting like a sieve straining out Ginsbergian howls that made her skin bubble like batter in a frying pan.

I saw her eyes smile. She was seated across from me alone, my father having disappeared, now hooked to his machine, his thorazine drip, the personalities,' laughter arranged like a house of cards, drifting to us like snow. The Virgin Islands, what a strange label, metaphor, the words painting a picture, *Salvador Dali's Vacation*. She would not or could not look at the word *virgin-* an embarrassment.

"More potatoes?" she looked at me, sad but afraid to cry.

I wanted to take her away, show her the sun always set in the west whether she believed it or not, but I knew she wouldn't go. All I could do was clean my plate and smile. It was all I knew how to do.

I found myself on the sidewalk, drifting toward the park. I hadn't remembered leaving the house. It was as if I'd awakened from a dream, sleepwalking. I found the swings, chains rusting, faded rubber seats dancing in the wind. I wanted to see if I could find the spirits, find the place they hung out. I was tired of being surprised, ambushed by their presence and my own thoughts. I wanted to have it out. I wanted them to explain to me what I had done. I wanted their forgiveness. I sat on the swing, rocking gently, the rings of the chain crying gently with each movement, a chorus of the damned. I closed my eyes and waited, feeling the rust crawl under the skin of my hands, turning me orange.

But no one came. I waited in the darkness, the sun having gone home. The lights of the neighborhood blinked like fireflies. Childhood seemed so far away, a lifetime ago, and yet when I began to think of the memories, they stretched to the beginning of time.

I heard the swing next to me move, the chains become taut, the squeak like a trapped mouse, and the breathing. I wanted to open my eyes, but I was afraid. I had chased them away before by knowing too much. Perhaps they had become shy, having lived in a different world where little is made of the future because there is none. I listened, and the breathing slowed. I could hear the heartbeat, a bass keeping the tempo while the electric self-accepted the notion of harmony, a jazz band tuning up. "Hi!"

I didn't want to open my eyes, to frighten them away, and have to start again. I didn't want to be forced to pray through weakness because it was the only thing I knew how to do; I knew there was no one home.

"Hi." The sound came again, accompanied by falling rust. It felt like molten snow on my skin, causing me to awaken as though thrown into the icy winter waters of the Mississippi. I recognized the voice. I got what I wished for; my mother had warned me about that. "Be careful what you wish for; you might just get it." I never understood until now. Once you accept the fact you are going to die, you should no longer be afraid. Being afraid of the inevitable is a waste of fear. And yet, I was afraid. I wanted to know why, but they refused to tell me. They knew, they had to know, and yet they wouldn't tell me.

The voice was unmistakable, although more cheerful than I remembered. I can't help but wonder if death doesn't agree with her. I might as well get it over with, fear or no fear; it is inevitable, I couldn't wait here forever pretending it would go away. My mother would eventually come looking for me. How would I explain?

I pulled myself upright and opened my eyes. Ralph sat next to me. He looked like he did in the picture, except he wore a tie with a fish on it; it glowed. "Don't listen to those morons." His voice sounded like Cecilia's. "They are just bored, pissed off really, because they can't have what you have. I know; I can't have it either." He began to swing, pulling hard on the chains, pointing his toes to the sky, leaning back, higher and higher, the chain popping as he reached the top of the arc.

I could understand Ralph's anger; after all, it was Cecilia who was responsible for his death, at least according to Butcher. I tend to not give too much credibility to people who have been wronged when they are extolling the virtues of the perpetrator. Also, I wasn't entirely sure with whom I was speaking. It looked like Ralph, well not the old Ralph but the new Ralph, but sounded exactly like Cecilia. Was this just another one of her tricks? Had Butcher put her up to this? Was he in on this conspiracy too? He and Cecilia working together. He was the one who'd told me about Cecilia's wish that I not delay too long.

Butcher told me once that the one thing he hated more than anything else was being alone. "I hate it," he'd said. "There's no friction. If there's no friction, there's no smoke, no fire, no light. It's like being in the dark with nothing to do, like being trapped in a coffin with nothing but your thoughts. That's why they started embalming people. They say it was because it preserved them so there could be services and visitations and all that, but it was really just to make sure they were dead. "You replace someone's blood with antifreeze and if they aren't dead, they soon will be, guaranteed." He was so melodramatic at times.

I couldn't believe Butcher, no matter how lonely he might be, would want to harm me in any way or even side with Cecilia, dead or not. He hated Catholic girls. "Stuck up bitches," he'd say. "Meanest tarts on the face of the earth." Butcher had had a neighbor girl who took care of him when he was little. He told me he could remember her being so sweet when his folks were there, Mr. This and Mrs. That, and then the minute they were gone, she'd lock him in his room and watch TV. He said she wouldn't even let him out to go to the bathroom. He said he'd had to pee out the window through the screen or wet his pants. He'd tried to tell his parents, but they wouldn't believe him.

Angela was such a pretty little thing, as his mother referred to her, and so sweet. He said his father only grunted and buried himself deeper in the newspaper. He said it wasn't until fall when the windows were closed and the heat turned on that they believed him. He said the urine soaked sill emitted an odor that would have brought tears to the eyes of a skunk. He got dropped off at his aunt's after that. He hated Catholic girls after that; I guess I don't blame him.

Sure we didn't see much of each other as we grew older, but memories soften with time, don't they, even if you're dead? I know if he'd lived, we'd be friends now; we would have gotten over whatever it was that had pulled us apart. We were best friends. He was the only one I could talk to.

"Hey, you should try this," he said in Cecilia's voice at the top of his arc. "It's just like dying." And then he was gone.

The swing's arc lessened, each time becoming progressively smaller. And then stillness settled in; just the memory of rust and the whimpering of the chain remained.

I saw him walking toward me, just a silhouette at first, unrecognizable. His stroll was one of confidence, a gunfighter walking in the dusty street, the mustached villain waiting. He took long strides, unnatural I thought, too athletic, too much like ballet, where their feet never touched the ground. He was sitting next to me on the swing, I didn't recognize him, but he seemed to know me. "You in some kind of trouble?" he asked. "I've been keeping an eye on you; a friend of yours asked if I'd do that. I don't have much to do, so I said I would. He seemed pleased."

"What friend?" I asked, knowing he'd not answer.

He look at me as though I knew who he meant but was afraid to believe. "So," he said in his gravelly voice, "what kind of trouble you in exactly?"

The figure next to me on the swing glowed slightly. I could make out his features in the darkness, although I couldn't see my own hand. He had long hair, longer than was the custom, and boots—black boots with small chains, silver, stretching across the top. He wore an overcoat even though it was summer and warm. He looked like Clint Eastwood, Bronco Billy; I hadn't cared for Westerns until then. He made me feel safe somehow, the way I'd always hoped my father would make me feel but never did. I looked but didn't see a gun, but then, even though he had his coat open and thrown back to his sides, it was a large coat. "You'd best tell me if you're going to before I forget why I'm here. I have trouble with that from time to time, staying focused I mean. So shoot," he said, raising his hand as though holding a gun and pointing it at me.

I knew he was an apparition, an illusion, a fantasy, but he was someone to talk to. What could it hurt? "I'm supposed to kill myself." I know I should have been subtler perhaps, but I'd said it, and there was no taking it back. I began to explain. I couldn't expect him to understand.

"This girl, she ..."

He interrupted. "Kill yourself? Supposed to? Please, go on." He threw one of his legs over the other and leaned back, holding onto the chains, his long hair touching the ground, his silver chains sparkling.

"This girl," I began again. "She told me—"

"This girl," he interrupted again and shook his head vigorously back and forth like a dog that had come out of the water. "What's she look like? I had a girlfriend, and not too long ago, she wanted me dead too. It kind of makes you reconsider the relationship. Yours anything like that?"

"No," I said more loudly than necessary. An old man looked at us from the sidewalk, his dog pulling him along. "No," I said more softly. "I didn't like her. I hardly knew her. She put a curse on me. She told me to go kill myself."

He said nothing. He straightened once more, placing both feet on the dirt; he placed one hand on his chin as if deep in thought. "This girl, was she a redhead, about five six, one eye slightly larger than the other?" He must have seen the frustration in my eyes for he suddenly slapped me on the back. "Only kidding, partner, only kidding. Now just tell me what it is I can do to help 'cause, frankly, I ain't got a clue."

I didn't need help; dying is something we all do on our own. Dying is more difficult than being born, primarily because we can't remember being born. We start out with a clean slate. It isn't until we get older, until we've had time to accumulate memories, that things become more complicated. I think the reason people fear death so much is because of the uncertainty of what comes next. We are told that God will welcome us to His kingdom where everything will be wonderful, where there will be no pain or suffering, no sorrow, only happiness. We want to believe, deep down I think we do, but we can't. Even the most devout believer seems to falter when the end approaches. We introduce doctrine, of course, that protects us like an umbrella from the hypocrisy of our faith. Even though death brings with it the greatest of rewards, we legislate for life as a sanctimonious state that must be preserved at all cost and with whatever machine necessary, except, of course, the electric chair, which is a machine reserved for the unfaithful.

We change the rules as we go along. We interpret obscure passages to mean what they must if we are to continue to cheat our own beliefs. We will do whatever it takes to outsmart ourselves when it comes to death because we do not trust ourselves to know what is right. Our minds attempt to reason with our own mortality in an effort to postpone that which we should gladly accept; and why? Because even though we profess our minds to be more closely affiliated with our spirits, we ultimately know our bodies have the final say. Our bodies will drag us kicking and screaming into the darkness because they are tired and they need to rest. They are worn out. They know the race is over and that no one wins, and yet our minds refuse to let go because they cannot ultimately believe their own lies. There is no magical kingdom, no yellow brick road, no Toto waiting at the end of a hard life to lick our faces and make it all better. There is only uncertainty and the conviction that death is inevitable.

"So," he said, reaching inside his coat, pulling out a flat-topped cowboy Stetson, placing it on his head, and tapping it slightly with his hand as if for luck. "So, you afraid to die?"

"No," I replied, "not afraid; just skeptical."

"How can you be skeptical about dying? Dying is dying. What did you expect—something different than what you know or believe? You don't believe in reincarnation, do you? You know reincarnation is a hell of a lot of fun to fool around with. I know. I enjoyed the hell out of it, but it goes nowhere, kid. It is like the perpetual motion machine or the car they are always going to invent that runs on water. It ain't going to happen. It's appealing, mind you. It does give us one more option then what we have now, assuming you're a Christian, but it's over the top. There's no end. Well that is not strictly true; there is an end, but it's so far down the road in the future that it's like trying to get a grip on eternity. I mean, for God's sakes, we are human beings. If it ain't simple, we ain't going to buy it."

I didn't want to argue with him, but I thought he was full of crap. I couldn't see a difference between any of the religions. They all promised something they could not deliver. They all had theories that could not be proven. They all had psychotic incidences that translated into divinity in one form or another. And last but not least, they had a bunch of the most gullible, frightened, uneducated subjects who were willing to believe anything but the truth. And the truth is that no one knows. We all have to die to find out.

If I had to choose between God and science, I'd put my money on science. Science gives us hope, where religion gives us fear. Life is energy. When life ends, the energy becomes some other form of energy. Sounds too simple to be ignored, and yet the Bible is the best-selling book in the world. Chemistry 101 has to be ordered from an obscure bookstore where someone with the name Hafinschlafinmaker has to order it for you. It is easier for us to believe whenwe we'll go to a place where our energy will be transformed, as if by some miracle, into another living thing and it won't take all eternity to do it. The next time you pick a flower you could be picking someone's great, great-grandfather; now that's scary.

"You don't seem to trust me,' he said, looking sideways at me as though he didn't want me to see the other side of his face. "Let me tell you something," he began, adjusting himself on the rubber seat, "These things aren't as uncomfortable as they look; they're worse." He wiggled slightly and continued, "It's like this. I feel like I'm on the runway. The plane has just left, and there I am standing there on the concrete not knowing what to do and feeling let down. Hell, life left me there. And then as I'm standing there, here comes this plane and it runs right over my foot, me standing there with my suitcase in my hand. Well the moral of the story, if there is one, is that it hurt like hell. Dead or not, it hurt like hell. You don't have to have a body to feel pain. You know that, don't you?" He turned away; all I could see was the back of his head. I think he was crying.

"I'm okay," I told him. "I really don't need your help."

"Hell, son, I know that. I've been following you around for a couple of weeks. You don't need help. You need someone to talk to. You need a girlfriend or something to take your mind off your troubles. I know a nice little redhead that—"

"No, that's okay. I'm fine." I wanted him to leave me alone. Company is a lot of work, and I just wasn't up to it.

"Kid, I know you don't need help. Your friend didn't send me here to help you. He sent me here for you to help me."

"What? What could I possibly help you with?"

He looked at me. I could tell he was somewhat disappointed by my reaction. Then I felt bad. Damn, sometimes I wish I didn't have feelings. I wish I could be cold, calculating like those gangsters who shoot someone and then sit down to have breakfast. But I can't. My mother said I inherited my grandmother's soft heart; my father says I inherited my grandfather's soft head.

Butcher had given me a book he'd found in a used bookstore. He said it would change my life. *Zen for the Complete Idiot*. He asked me several times if I'd read it, and I kept saying I hadn't gotten to it yet. And then one day, he said if I hadn't read it by Friday, he wanted it back. Butcher wasn't the kind of guy to give ultimatums, so I thought there might actually be something to this book.

So I began to read it, I couldn't put it down. It had nothing to do with Zen; it was a book about psychology. The preface is a confession by the author that pretty much says he picked the title as a way to get people's attention. "I wanted to make a few bucks. Writing seemed like a simple way to do it; beats digging graves. But I had nothing to say, so I made up a title that sounded interesting, and seeing how that went pretty well, I made up the rest."

The book was fascinating because it was all made up. Better than Freud. The more inventive he became, the more like Freud I became until he started wearing false beards and writing anonymous love notes to his mother. She enjoyed them, he said; the beard gave him a rash. It was a truly inspirational book because the more irrational it became, the more real it became. Anyway, the moral to his little story was that the only difference between fantasy and reality was the $22.50 the book had cost. He closed, "I made a few dollars, and I thank you."

The book primarily goes into the art of psychoanalysis, which the author translates to mean knowing which questions to ask and how to ask them. In chapter three, "It's All about Questions," he explains that a good psychoanalyst is merely a fortune teller with a degree. You learn to ask the right questions, give the answers, they are cured, you are a genius, and everyone goes home happy. I thought I'd give it a try. My cowboy looked so unhappy, and not because he was dead. "So," I began. In *Zen for the Complete Idiot*, the author always began with the word *so*. He said it was one of those words that was not only an icebreaker but a transition, which formed the bond necessary for a truly moving bullshit session. "So, what happened? So how did you end up dead?"

He looked surprised, as if he'd thought I hadn't realized he was dead. "I didn't duck."

"You didn't duck? Could you be a bit more specific?"

"No, not really. I don't remember much of what happened. It all happened so quickly. I didn't feel any pain. I just woke up dead."

"Could you explain waking up dead?"

"One minute, I was alive; the next thing I knew, I wasn't."

"Oh."

Being dead wasn't as easy as the book made it out to be. Possibly if the author would have been a bit more empathetic, but I could tell he was embarrassed by the whole thing. "So," I continued, "what were you doing prior to waking up dead? Perhaps it will give us some clues."

He liked my suggestion; he smiled, pushing his hat back on his head to expose his forehead, white as new linen and smooth. One thing I had noticed of late was how wonderful the complexion of dead people is, perfect.

"I was a professional caddy." I could see he was proud of having been a professional caddy. He sat up straight and looked me right in the eye. "Professional tour." He smiled as though he'd never been as happy.

"Go on," I said. "Please continue. And by the way, what is a professional caddy?"

He looked at me like I had just gotten off the boat from New Jersey. "Golf," he said. "Golf."

"Oh," I said. "Oh, please continue. Sorry."

"That's all right," he said, continuing to look at me to see if maybe I was putting him on. "When you caddy for these pros, you learn to keep your eyes on the ball; keep your mouth shut; and, most importantly, always wear earplugs. It cuts down on the distractions, making it easier to keep your eye on the ball and your mouth shut. You know how they are always yelling fore, so people watch out when they hit a ball where they're not supposed to? Did you know that the odds of being hit by a golf ball while standing along the fairway is four million two hundred and eighty-six to one? I got to where I didn't look up anymore. After I got the earplugs, I didn't even know when I was supposed to look up. Life was simple then.

"One day, to cut the story short, I was in the second day of a tournament. My guy was doing okay; we'd be in it the next day for sure, which meant money in my pocket. I was feeling blessed if you know what I mean. I was counting my chickens before they hatched. I was, in fact, doing what I shouldn't have been doing, daydreaming. I wasn't paying attention. I wasn't focused. I stepped right into the path of one of the hardest swinging golfers on the tour. *Whack.* Number one wood, right in the temple. I don't remember much of it. They say I died almost instantly. I don't know what they did with my share of the money."

I wondered if he was telling the truth. The dying part is easy; your brain ceases to function, your body dies—end of story. "But what is there between the golf club and waking up dead? That is what I want you to help me with. That is the part I can't figure out, can't logically extrapolate from fact."

"Why do you want to know? What is the point? It's like trying to explain the difference between black and white to a blind man. It isn't relevant until you need it to be; it isn't relevant until you are dead." He lowered his chin onto his chest and closed his eyes as though exhausted.

We sat in silence, him gently rocking, the chains screaming in muffled agony, the rust falling like orange snow.

"Do you know," he said, continuing to keep his eyes closed, "how lucky you are? You know how to ask questions. Most of the people I knew back then and most I come across now don't know how to ask questions. They not only don't know how, they don't want to know how. They are afraid of the answers. Do you know that the majority of people are more afraid of sin than of guilt? And they are one and the same thing. It is impossible to have one without the other. What you really want to know from me is what it is like to be dead? Am I wrong? Being dead, if you must know, is no different than being alive; it just happens in a different place, a place where guilt doesn't exist because guilt has no value. If you want to know what heaven is like, or hell, I can't give you an answer. It would be like trying to explain the difference between good light and bad light. There is no difference; the only real connection is that you are able to use one where you cannot the other. You are able to benefit from one and not the other.

"I have a riddle for you. What do a Seeing Eye dog and a white cane have in common?"

I waited, assuming he would continue.

"They both need a blind master to be relevant; otherwise, there is only a stick and a dog." The cowboy pretended to laugh, "You don't think it's funny?"

I didn't want to hurt his feelings, but he knew.

"I had a family, did I tell you that?"

He looked at me again with those hollow eyes, lonely, not because he was alone—he could accept that—but because he wanted to be alone. "Yes, I had a family. The usual family, wife, kids. Is that what you mean? Funny thing, when I had it, I didn't know what to do with it. And now that I don't have it, I miss it. Families are like molecular experiments. You never know where they are going to end up—saving someone's life, saving the world, or destroying everything you know and love. I was afraid of my life, my family, and my kids. I was afraid of everything, but most of all, I was afraid of myself. And they were afraid of me too. I didn't know that until it was too late, till after I woke up dead. You find out a lot of things, after you're dead, that you wish you knew when you, well, weren't dead.

"My kids were afraid of me—not because I was mean to them but because they didn't know who I was. It's like being afraid of a stranger. And we are all strangers really, all of us. We don't know anyone really, don't know ourselves. People look up in the sky and see a bunch of ducks flying north and see only migration, a bunch of ducks flying because they have been programmed to do so—flying together because it is the way they survive. It doesn't mean they understand one another or even understand why they do the things they do. They just do them.

"And I was afraid of my kids. They scared the crap out of me. They needed me to love them, and I didn't know how. They needed my advice, and I didn't know how to give it to them. We were like oil and water, not because we had to be but because we wanted to be. We were afraid of being ourselves. How screwed up is that? And yet it happens every day in every city, in every state, in every country, and it cannot end because we are afraid to let it, because if it does, it will make us take a good look at who and what we are. And what will we do when we don't like what we see?"

"So what you're saying is that we are some giant experiment that never works out? We will go on hurting one another for all eternity? We will go on blaming the devil because it is easier than looking our families in the eye and telling them we are scared shitless? You don't have to tell me that. You don't have to tell me I'm scared shitless. I know I am. You need to tell me there's a way out. I need to know there is some hope, a chance if nothing else. You've begun to piss me off. If life is an experiment that doesn't work out and death is no more than reliving a failed experiment, then why are you here? Did they send you to rub salt in the wound, to tell me I'm damned if I do and damned if I don't? I know that already. Tell me something I can use, tell me something that might help me make a difference."

He began to fade, as the fog fades when the sun rises, burning away the water that has attached itself to the air because it has nothing better to do. I wanted to hug him, tell him everything would be different, but

I couldn't. I didn't believe it myself. And then he was gone, my cowboy, like smoke in the wind, gone. It was dark once more, darker than I ever remembered it being, and I was cold, colder than I had ever been. He hadn't even said good-bye.

I wondered if it were possible to wake up alive. Being dead wasn't very educational. I've learned more from cereal boxes.

I watched the old man and the dog return, walking slowly, the dog sniffing and pulling the old man down the walk, giving his life purpose. There must be a time when you know, when you realize you are no longer needed, an old whore hanging on because that is all you know. It hurts to walk, is impossible to crawl, and you are unwilling to beg. There must come a time when even the unknown is more appealing than the known.

I had seen her behind the tree, just a portion of her face, but enough; she was singing. She must have thought I hated singing, but I don't. It is the one indulgence we should afford ourselves outside the shower.

I slipped from the swing as she sang *Heaven, just like Heaven*, her voice off-key and sharp, grating like chalk on a board, and yet beautiful because the words carry the tune like a wounded soldier across the battlefield to safety.

"Cecilia, Cecilia," I call.

She pretends not to hear.

"Come out, come out wherever you are," I goaded her to come forth into the light, for the game must end; life is too short. I could no longer settle for the gold watch at the end of fifty years, the honorariums, the accolades. They were but words and, unless written in the heavens where one has no option but to look, of what good were words? Lives, like lint, hiding under the bed waiting to be sucked up by the newest version of Hoover, HEPA.

"I would no longer wish to be remembered for the poem I wrote, the letter I delivered, or the country I saved, because it all means nothing unless it means something to me. Your medals, credentials, and money mean something only if they mean something to you. Leave me alone, so that I might not only die in peace but also live in peace. Leave me alone so that I might fight the demons that need to be fought. It is my choice, my life, my death, and no one else'choice, Cecilia.

"Please step from behind the tree if you are not afraid of life; step from behind the tree and let me see you. Step from behind the tree dressed in white, the symbol of purity, and let me see the guilt stains upon it; I have learned a way to remove the stains. Tell me why your death can only be justified by mine. Tell me why I have been cursed, because like Judas, I am only human and feel that I have been wrongly accused. A god should not fault those of lesser status, for it is those of lesser status who make him God. If He were so inclined to influence me, then let Him speak in that mighty voice of His that caused Moses to see bushes on fire and writing on stones. Let Him know that, without us, He would not exist, except in His own eyes, and that is a lonely existence indeed."

I watch the small figure step from behind the tree, still humming to herself. The veil was pulled over her eyes, and she held what I assumed to be a prayer book in her hand. Her black shoes glistened in the light from the corner post. She stood looking at me from across the street, not moving. I waited; she seemed to remain frozen in the darkness, her humming becoming louder. I remembered the tune. I watched as her gloved hand raised and, with her finger, she beckoned me to come.

I didn't want to go—fear, I suppose. But then the anguish of the past years washed over me. I needed to end this once and for all. I needed to talk with her, find out what it was that she needed from me—what I needed to do to break the spell so that I might live without someone else's shadow.

She remained motionless, arm extended. She had raised her finger and motioned me to come. As I stepped from the curb, the asphalt turned to a river. The water, soon rushing over my knees, hindered each step farther. I took one step, two, and yet she seemed to grow no closer. The street appeared to widen, a black asphalt river widening with each step. She began to smile; her hand now dropped to her side. I continued to walk, now attempting to run, dragging each foot through the turbulent waters as her distance widened from me. She raised her hand once more, this time waving as though she were leaving. Or was I? Her smile widened as the lights from the car encapsulated her in a halo's brilliance. She held tight to the book, taking a measure of peace from its beautifully bound, red leather cover with the gold embossed letters now glistening in the light—Dante's *Divine Comedy*.

I watched the lights as they searched the darkness like a nocturnal hunter seeking its prey. The bright eyes seemed to glow as they made their way first from one side of the widening river to the other. I attempted to return to the boulevard, but my legs, hampered by the rushing blackness, did little but march in place. The eyes found me after much searching and widened as if in anticipation, and it drew closer, seemingly satisfied that, as the pickings were scarce, I would do. The lights moved quickly, its cones fixed, no longer wavering, causing me to shield my eyes from the glare.

I wasn't frightened; nor was I surprised. I turned from the lights to where Cecilia had stood. She was gone. What appeared to be a shoe lay next to the tree. As the car drew closer, the license plate loomed like a billboard, "PIG 63." The lights separated as the car, now only a few feet away, revealed its occupants. Butcher, his large, black-rimmed glasses resting on the tip of his nose, he peered through the web of the steering wheel. Beads of sweat lined his forehead, his short red hair at attention, his face glowing with excitement as our eyes met. Ralph was sitting next to the window, his dog in his lap, its head protruding from the passenger window, barking as though warning me of the inevitability of my circumstance. Cecilia sat in the middle, her veil now raised, clutching her book to her chest, her white gloves obliterating the embossed, gold letters. She was smiling; the last thing I saw was her smile broadening as the car struck me.

I do not remember pain or regret. I didn't feel anything except a peacefulness that flowed over me and through me, leaving me exhausted, a numbness I had not experienced before. I don't know what I expected, never having died before. But it was different than what I could have imagined. There were no angels, no trumpets, and no tunnel with a bright light coaxing me to the far end. It was dark; dark, the total absence of light. I couldn't have seen my hand in front of my face if I'd had a hand. It wasn't frightening. Not once did anxiety creep into my thoughts. If I was disappointed by anything, it would have been that there was no one to greet me, no one to help me across to the other side. I was alone, which I had been wishing for my entire life; the irony made me laugh.

Quiet was the other thing besides the darkness that I hadn't expected. There was absolutely no sound. It is not the silence of an empty room, for a room has memory; a room has possibility. It is the silence of a tomb, designed for an eternity of peace. It is what I had imagined outer space to be like. I could only exist in the darkness and quiet and think about what would come next.

I have believed in the theory that energy could not be created or destroyed, and therefore, when we died our energy changed form; it was as simple as that. I was, for all practical purposes, a bodiless spoonful of energy in the quiet dark. And then what? I couldn't think of anything. I thought of going in search of Butcher, but where to begin? Ralph had obviously found his dog, so it was possible, and Cecilia had found me. I couldn't help but wonder if it was worth it, and yes, I had to come to the conclusion that it was. No matter what, no matter how short my time on earth had been, I'd had my chance. I had something to compare everything else to. Without life, light has no meaning, sound can't be imagined, and people, though most of them are not who they pretend to be, do bring a sense of belonging to one's life.

I lay here, wherever here is, for a few seconds or perhaps half of eternity; I have no idea of a future. Future must have a beginning and an end; eternity denies both. Everything no longer has relevance, and I can't help … help … The sound pulls me from oblivion, it is growing louder, waves lapping at the shore, an invasion onto the sand, and then retreating in silence.

A siren? It sounds like a siren, an arrow piercing the darkness, the quiet; and now I feel the eyes of destiny burning, searching my soul for signs of …

Voices, faint, far off grow more defined and louder. Voices? Death is not at all what I expected.

My sense of smell is also returning, I smell wet dog. "God spelled backward," as Butcher was fond of saying. He used to kid me about Catholics not being able to spell, let alone spell backward. I couldn't help but think Butcher was coming to rescue me, carry me from the darkness, from the silence, the enemy of youth. The voices louder, at first no more than a whisper, and then I recognized a voice from the past, Butcher's. I wanted to call to him. I wanted to wave as though lost in a sea of black grass—*Here I am. I'm over here.* But I could not bring myself to conjure hope from the futility surrounding me. What good would it do? I was gone; calling for help was no longer an option, no more than a prayer.

I do not believe in heaven or hell for that matter. I could never understand the fascination with the mystical places that would entomb us in happiness or sorrow, perhaps both, perhaps neither; our essence floating in the universe alone for all eternity. Perhaps we are destined to be alone with our doubts, fears, and unanswered prayers, and …

I hear it again, louder this time. It is Ralph's voice and faint barking coming from the darkness, the primeval call of a dog.

*"Hey. Hey!" The words force themselves into my consciousness. "Hey, you all right?"*

*All right? All right with what? Was it all right that the game was over and I'd lost? Was it all right I'd never get a chance to say good-bye? What was all right?*

*"Hey." The words again, slipping past my disappointment. Butcher's voice. "Hey, open your eyes."*

*I could feel a hand on my shoulder, shaking me.*

*I opened my eyes, and the darkness turned to gray and then disappeared—gone. The air teemed with the sounds of the city, the playground. The sky was a blurry brilliance, the billowing white clouds painted onto a blue background. Faces looking down at me, although I could barely make them out, faces, I was sure of it.*

*I blinked trying to chase the glaze from my eyes; the faces, water color portraits ran together, becoming illusions of what I wanted so much to see. Then slowly, they became clearer, and finally I recognized Butcher's face, the gym bars stretched above him, a bridge with no beginning and no end. And Ralph, and Cecilia! Her face was no longer drawn and thin; she was dressed in her plaid school uniform looking down at me with a look of wonder in her eyes.*

*"I thought you were dead," she offered softly, her words no more than a whisper; she turned and disappeared onto the asphalt. She was missing a shoe.*